CALLED TO DUTY
BOOK 1

Doug Murray

CALLED TO DUTY
BOOK 1

DOUBLE DRAGON

A DOUBLE DRAGON PAPERBACK

ISBN 978-1-78695-436-7

Double Dragon
is an imprint of
Fiction4All

Published 2020
Fiction4All
www.fiction4all.com

PROLOGUE

ANBAR PROVINCE

It had been a long and difficult mission—long enough and tiring enough for SFC Robert Piper to grab some sleep in the back of his team's truck rather than ride in the usual shotgun slot in front.

That decision saved his life.

Piper was sound asleep when the IED went off, lifting the front end of the truck nearly ten feet into the air while a hail of makeshift shrapnel killed the driver and the SPEC-4 who'd taken Piper's seat.

When the bomb went off, Piper was having a pleasant dream about home and Lisa, the woman he'd loved since they'd first met in High School. He'd found a spot at the very back of the truck that had enough room for his six foot four inch frame to sprawl out. That meant that when the front of the truck lifted into the air, Piper was dropped—quite rudely—into the middle of a deadly ambush.

"What the hell!" He bellowed as he smashed into the hot asphalt of the roadway, barely conscious of the truck cartwheeling away from him. He bounced and slid, still cursing, until his body slammed into the berm of hard packed sand that formed the edge of the roadbed.

Instantly he found himself under fire.

Insurgents with an IED got the truck! He realized as, now fully awake, he rolled away from the bullets impacting the asphalt all around him.

He low-crawled over the berm, putting a little cover between him and the enemy fire, crouching behind that very tentative shelter, he turned to see what had happened to the rest of his team…

Just as his truck bounced one last time before striking the berm on the opposite side of the road. It punched halfway through before sliding to a halt in a more or less upright position.

Its front end, he noted, was mangled beyond recognition.

I've got to see if anyone else survived! Piper thought as he stared at what was left of the truck. Although I'm not sure how that could have happened…

Piper popped up over the berm long enough to have a look around before being forced duck back down by a new flurry of gunfire.

Those've gotta be the ragheads who set off the IED, he groped around for his rifle—but found that the lanyard designed to secure it to his body armor had been shredded at some point in his travels.

The M-4 was gone.

Great! He drew his handgun and jacked a round into the chamber. Now where are those…?

He ducked low and tried to push himself under the sand as another flurry of gunfire came from above.

He could feel the bullets slam into the sand around him.

This is not good, he thought, eyeing the rise that ran alongside the road. They've got the high ground and automatic weapons! I have… He looked at his Browning. This!

He turned toward the truck, hoping against hope that just one of his squad had survived, if they had, there might be a chance…

He heard a noise from what was left of the truck—a rustling sound followed by the appearance of a familiar face...

Gianelli! The RTO still had the radio strapped to his back—but he wasn't trying to use it—he wasn't trying to do anything more than fight his way clear of the truck.

He looks dazed, Piper thought. I don't think he's really aware of what's going on—instinct is pushing him toward the light. Piper's eyes widened with shock when Gianelli, using his right hand only, pushed his chest and head free of the truck—and rolled forward and out—revealing what was left of him.

God! Piper's eyes widened. His left arm is completely gone! Piper stared at the man. It must have been sheared off by the blast. He watched as Gianelli struggled to be free of the truck. He's bleeding pretty badly—it's a miracle he's still alive!

A moment later, Gianelli half-jumped, half-fell from the back of the truck and into the sand below. He pushed himself upright, barely able to stand, before staggering unsteadily away from the wreck.

He took one step, two steps...

Gunfire exploded from the top of the rise—a lot more than before. There are more shooters up there now, Piper realized. Their leader must have called for reinforcements...

He heard a bullet spang off Gianelli's body armor; another hit him in left leg.

Blood exploded from the wound...

Gianelli cried out mindlessly and fell to the ground. He tried to get back on his feet, tried to crawl forward—and found he couldn't move.

Crying, he gave up; rolling himself into a fetal position, arm in front of his eyes as he tried to hide.

The insurgents did not take pity on the wounded man. They kept firing, hitting the Gianelli again and again. The RTO cried like a baby as he was hit in the legs over and over ...

He screamed when one well-aimed shot hit him squarely in the groin—and was silenced an instant later as an AK-47 round hit him in the head...

Piper shook his head in disbelief and horror. The man had barely managed to clear the remains of the truck before he had been—quite literally—shot to pieces.

I might have saved him if I had been able to give him cover fire; Piper looked at the unmoving body of the youngster who had served with him for months. But with my rifle gone, I couldn't even do that!

He shook his head and took a moment to check the load on his Browning. I can't do much for myself, either.

Then he realized that the squad radio—the PRC-117F—was still strapped to the dead man's back.

It looks like it might be intact, he thought for a long moment. If I can reach it—and if it works—I might be able to call in an airstrike...

More gunfire sounded from the hillside above. The insurgents had apparently decided that Piper couldn't escape from his position so, having seen Gianelli crawl out of the truck, they'd decided it would be smart to make sure there were no other survivors.

The canvas top of the five ton rippled from the impact of round after round of AK-47 ammo…

I've got to get to that radio, Piper decided. If I stay here, they'll come down on my flanks…

He waited until the fire slowed.

They're reloading, he took a deep breath, got a firm grip on his handgun…

And made a full-speed dash for the truck.

The sudden and unexpected move took the gunmen on the ridge by surprise. It took nearly three full seconds for them to react—more than enough time for Piper to slide behind the tires on the right hand side of the truck.

Okay! He pulled himself into a ball, tight enough to use the thick rubber and metallic belt of the tire as a shield against the insurgent fire. If these guys continue to show their usual lack of fire discipline…

They did—the insurgents kept firing at full automatic, spraying and praying that they'd get a hit.

AK-47's on automatic chew up ammunition at a rate of about a hundred rounds a minute. Piper knew that the insurgents always fired on automatic and would run their magazines dry in a very short time. He stayed under cover and waited until the firing sputtered to an halt before making his move. I hope nobody up there saved a few rounds...

Firing his pistol blindly toward the men on the hill (hoping to keep their heads down), Piper scrambled out from behind the tires and grabbed the webbing that held the radio on Gianelli's back.

He didn't intend—and had no time—to undo the buckles and snaps that held it in place. Instead, he emptied what was left of his magazine in the insurgents' direction and dragged the RTO's body back behind the cover of the big tire.

He had just gotten beside the body when the insurgents completed their reload and opened fire again...

Now let's see if this was worth the effort, he steeled himself and unbuckled the radio, pulling it away from his dead friend's back. If this thing took a hit ...

He made a quick inspection. Found no holes, no obvious dents...

It seems okay. He rested the radio against the back of the massive tire sheltering him and switched it on, picking up the headset as soon as he saw the dials light up...

"Rainbow Echo Five Five," he spoke as clearly as he could. "I say again, Rainbow Echo Five Five is requesting immediate assistance. My vehicle is disabled and I am under fire..."

"Rainbow Echo Five Five, this is Hunter One Niner. The return transmission was strong and clear. "State position, over."

"I am on Highway 80—that is Highway eight-zero somewhere between Mosul and Al Khidhir," Piper paused. "Can't give it to you finer than that— I was asleep when the truck took the hit."

"Roger Rainbow Echo Five Five," the voice seemed unperturbed. "I have a GPS fix on your radio and an asset in the air." A pause. "Three minutes out—can you hold on?"

"Yeah," Piper nodded. "I've got good cover and..." He checked his remaining magazines.

"Thirty rounds of ammo—that should last me three minutes."

"Roger, stay on the line and I will let you know when the asset is approaching."

"Roger Hunter One Niner," Piper took in a deep breath. "And many thanks."

"Don't thank me, man." The other's voice seemed amused. "Thank the boys at 'General Atomics' who built the damn Predators—I don't think there's anything else in the area that could reach you in time."

"Roger that," Piper took a quick look up the rise—the insurgents were still there. "Although I'll be happy to buy you a cold one if I get out of this."

"I'll hold you to that." The other man chuckled. "One minute. Give me your exact position."

"I am sheltering under what's left of a five ton truck on the south side of the highway—the Insurgents are on the North side of the road on top of a rise."

"Roger that," there was a long pause. "I see them now." Another pause. "Stay down..."

The top of the ridge suddenly exploded in smoke, flame, and dust.

"Looks like a good hit with the Hellfire," Piper heard. "Stay down while I make a strafing run..."

"Strafing run?" Piper frowned. "I thought you were flying a Predator, they can't..."

Piper stopped in mid-sentence as bullets hit just to his right. He ducked away, the Browning automatically coming up into firing position...

And saw four insurgents—each armed with an AK-47—approaching from his right.

I guess they got bored! He realized. And realized that I wasn't going to give them a clear shot He flicked the safety off the Browning. So they decided to try to flank me!

He dropped the pistol's sights onto the closest man's chest. Wish I had a rifle… And squeezed the trigger.

The target jolted to a stop so suddenly he might have run into a wall, and then crumpled to the ground in a heap.

Piper nodded to himself. As long as they just spray and pray and don't stop to aim…

He fired again—and the second man dropped in his tracks, blood spurting from his forehead.

One of the two survivors began shouting orders and broke to one side.

They're going to try to take me from both sides. Piper thought. I'll go for the leader first… He tracked the man running to his right, allowed his finger to take first pressure on the trigger…

Thunder sounded in the sky behind him as the drone made a second run, this time firing a minigun that Piper could see was in a weapons pod slung beneath a wing.

The two surviving insurgents barely had time to look up before dozens of 30mm depleted uranium rounds chewed them into bloody chunks…

A moment later, the Predator banked and made a long strafing run along the ridge line, scattering bloody bits of insurgent in all directions.

The fight was over.

"I think you're clear now," the voice on the radio told him. "I have a medevac on the way and I'll orbit the site until it gets there."

"Roger that," Piper nodded. "One question."

"Ask."

"What's your name?"

The man chuckled. "Farrell," the voice told him. "Franklyn Fitzgerald Farrell."

"Alright, Mr. Farrell," Piper grinned. "I'll be looking to get you that drink!"

"And I'll be waiting." There was a short pause. "Chopper on approach now—good luck, Sergeant."

"How do you know I'm a Sergeant?"

"I'm CIA," Farrell chuckled. "I have your file in front of me right this minute."

"What does it say?"

"It says that I should be the one offering you a drink—and a job."

"I might take you up on both," Piper looked at Gianelli's lifeless body. "I'm getting kind of tired of the one I have now."

***

The Medevac chopper didn't wait to pick up the bodies of Piper's men—a truck from graves registration was already on the way to take care of that unhappy chore and the pilot had orders to fly Piper directly to Camp Freedom for a meeting with higher command—and the pilot had enough experience not to keep the brass waiting.

"Why do they want to talk to me?" Piper asked the warrant officer flying the Apache. "I mean, I expected to go through a debrief but figured I'd have time to get a shower and a change of clothing…"

"No clue," the pilot shrugged. "All I know is that I was ordered to get you back as quickly as possible—no loitering, no delays, and no excuses."

13

"Crap," Piper began thinking of ways he might have screwed up. Are they pissed that I wasn't in the front seat of the truck? He frowned at the thought. Was there some kind of 'instruction' on that I missed? He didn't know and, as Camp Freedom's helipad loomed ahead, he knew he wouldn't have time to look it up—if he had any idea of where to look. All he could do was wait and see what was to come...

***

"You're Piper?" The man who met him at the helicopter door was short and wiry; with hair long enough to mark him as a civilian despite the cammo fatigues identical to Piper's—albeit fatigues that were clean and sans insignia of any kind.

"I am," the sergeant looked the man up and down. "Who are you?"

A smile split the other man's face as he stuck out a hand. "Farrell's the name—Frank Farrell." the grin widened. "We sort of met a little while ago..."

"Mr. Farrell!" Piper took the offered hand and gave it a firm shake. "Glad to meet you," he grinned. "I guess this is about that drink?"

"Not just yet," the shorter man nodded toward a Humvee parked at the edge of the helipad. "You need to report in first—I came to give you a quick debrief," he shrugged. "And a warning."

"Warning?"

"Yeah," Farrell climbed into the Humvee's driver seat and motioned Piper to join him. "First, you should know that the brass is going to present you with the Silver Star for your recent action."

"I didn't do anything..."

14

"Of course you did," Farrell put the vehicle into gear and spun the steering wheel. "You killed nine insurgents single-handedly," he glanced at Piper. "With nothing but a handgun!"

"The Predator…"

"Oh, you did get a little help from the drone's missile," Farrell gave him a hard look. "Just the missile because there was nothing else the drone could do…"

"But the strafing run…"

"Predator's don't have guns," Farrell looked at Piper. "You know that."

"I don't understand…"

"I'll give you a full explanation later—when we have that drink. For now, just keep the story straight—you killed the insurgents the Hellfire didn't get. You and you alone." Farrell held up his index finger in a rather pedantic gesture. "There was no strafing run—no minigun mounted on a drone-- nothing unusual at all. You got some help from a Hellfire missile." He raised an eyebrow. "The rest was all you."

The Sergeant nodded slowly. "Yeah, I got it."

"Good," Farrell halted the Humvee in front of a large prefabricated building. "I believe this is your headquarters—just smile and take the medal—your wife will be proud of you."

"Yeah," Piper nodded. "So will my son."

"You've got a boy?"

"Sean," Piper smiled. "He's almost ten."

"You're a lucky man," Farrell slapped him on the back. "A hero with a pretty wife and a son— what more could you ask for?"

"More information?"

15

"Later." Farrell nodded toward the door. "After they finish blowing smoke up your ass."

"Where should I meet you?"

"Don't worry about it," Farrell smiled. "I'm your ride—I'll be right here when you're done."

Piper nodded and climbed out of the Humvee—which pulled away the instant he slammed the door closed. I'm not supposed to talk about Drones with chain guns, he nodded to himself. Okay, OK—Farrell saved my life so I owe it to him to play along. He watched the Humvee turn toward the far side of the base. But I'll expect a hell of an explanation when we have that drink! He stretched, checked his uniform, and headed for the headquarters door, automatically straightening his shoulders as he went.

And Mr. Farrell is definitely the one who'll be doing the buying!

***

Farrell did buy—but not at the NCO club that Piper frequented. Instead, the shorter man drove them to a very well-appointed bar on the far side of the base where a pretty girl took their order.

"What is this place?" Piper looked around. "I never heard anything about an O-Club in this quadrant."

"It's a private club," Farrell smiled. "Civilian contractors..." His smile widened. "And their guests, of course."

"So I'm your guest?"

Farrell nodded before leaning forward. "How did your debrief go?"

"Nobody asked anything about armed drones, if that's what you're asking," Piper told him. "They

16

just talked about what a great job I did and how proud they all are." He looked at his companion. "They let me talk to my wife—already had her on the phone when I walked in."

"Nice of them."

"Yeah, nice." Piper nodded slowly. "Now why don't you tell me about what you're doing here— and how do you come to have impossibly-armed Predator drones."

"Okay," Farrell took a quick look around. "First, as I told you back there, I'm not some damn contractor—I'm CIA."

"Yeah, I remember that."

"I'm here to test a new generation of Predators—drones that are far more mission-capable than the ones we've been using up to now."

"Drones with guns and missiles?"

"And some other things I can't talk about right now."

"Okay," Piper sat back while the pretty girl returned and placed a bottle, two glasses, and a bucket of ice in front of them. When she was gone, he leaned forward, eyes fixed on those of his companion. "What can you talk about?"

"My superiors have had a look at the footage from today's little escapade—they think you might be a good addition to our team."

"Me?" Piper's brow creased. "In the CIA?"

"Why not?" Farrell smiled. "We need all kinds of men—and I think you'd be a real asset. You have a good rep as a leader and a better one as a shooter."

"Why me?"

"I've been through your packet—you have a BA in history and an AA in computer science." He looked at Piper, eyes narrow. "Which forces me to ask you: Why are you here?"

The soldier poured a drink and took a sip. "Good stuff."

"Nothing but the best." Farrell filled his own glass. "And you haven't answered my question."

"I'm not sure I can." Piper finished his drink, poured another. "It's complicated…"

"I know that your father was career military—I also know that he was in the Khobar Towers when they were bombed…"

Piper nodded.

"So you felt you had to, what, avenge him?"

"Not exactly," the tall soldier emptied his refilled glass. "I did sort of feel like…" He shrugged. "I felt like I owed him and the others with him something…"

"That's stupid."

"Yeah," Piper grinned. "I know, but…"

"But you still have to do it." Farrell looked him in the eye. "How does your wife feel about it?"

"Lisa knew all about me when we got married—she's okay with it…"

"Really?" Farrell shook his head. "She's happy with that shithole of an apartment? Happy with that beat-up car she's driving?"

"She's a soldier's wife…"

"She doesn't have to be." The CIA man poured a second drink. "I can give you the same salary as a GS-13…"

"How much is that?"

"Just over Seventy grand a year." He looked at Piper. "You can get a decent house, a nice car…"

"You're serious about this?"

"Dead serious." Farrell looked Piper squarely in the eye. "Say yes and you leave here tomorrow."

"Going where?"

"The Farm—it's where the CIA sends new people for their version of basic training." Farrell smiled. "I don't think you'll have any difficulty graduating."

Piper thought for a long moment, the faces of Gianelli and the rest of his now-dead team running through his mind's eye, then…

"Okay," he held out his hand. "I think you have a new recruit."

"Good," Farrell shook. "It'll be good to have someone I know I can trust in the field with me…"

***

HELMAND PROVINCE, AFGHANISTAN—2 YEARS LATER

"Who chose this spot for a listening post?" Piper shouted into his earbud. "There are two Taliban camps within a half-mile!"

"Just a little mistake," Farrell's voice was low and clear in Piper's ear. "I depended on surveillance information given to me by our friends in Kabul."

Piper grunted.

"Okay, I was wrong to trust them! We can argue about it when you get back."

"Yeah—and all I have to do is take out thirty or forty Taliban fighters before I get clear enough for a pick-up."

"There are way more than that!" Farrell's tone was almost jovial. "I've got a satellite over you right now—and it shows a second large party of Taliban just to the east of your present position."

"Wonderful!"

"We can handle it—pull back to..." He shuffled some papers in front of him. "Charlie Five on your map. Lots of cover there—fort up and wait."

"How long," Piper motioned for his party to move in the indicated direction. "And what are we waiting for?"

"The cavalry of course," Farrell's voice was amused. "I have two Predators and a Reaper enroute to your location. They'll be overhead in three mikes."

"You're gonna use us as the anvil for your little drone hammers, aren't you?"

"Why not? The bad guys are going to do their best to run you down no matter what I do and that position in Charlie Five has lots of cover." He paused. "You and your team still have plenty of ammo, right?"

"Right."

"Then just grab some cover, keep your head down, and wait. The drones will do all the hard work."

"You have a lot of confidence in those damned drones."

"They've saved you more than once!"

"I guess..." Piper muttered as he led his men through a lightly wooded area and up a slope that led to the position Farrell had indicated. "How're the others doing?"

"Team Four picked up four senior commanders—they'll have the bastard's enroute to Gitmo by the time you get back to base."

"Gitmo?" Piper held up a hand to stop his men, eyes studying the lay of the land in front of him. "I thought the whole idea of taking those guys prisoner was to get Intel? We're not going to get that in Gitmo—maybe at one of the black sites..."

"Maybe," Farrell chuckled. "But our masters are busy playing politics right now. Abu Ghraib burned a lot of bridges for the Administration so they think it's safer to just stick them in Gitmo—out of the way—until things blow over and we can try something else."

"That makes no sense at all." Piper started pointing his men to picked positions. "We might as well just let them go."

"Not our call," Farrell hesitated. "No talk now—just get your guys under cover as quickly as you can. One of the Taliban groups has reached the base of the hill and is starting up."

"Roger that," Piper positioned the last of his men and took the spot he'd decided would be his own. "Make sure your 'cavalry' isn't too late."

"It won't be."

"Good," Piper laid the red dot of his sight onto the chest of a man just appearing at the edge of their position. "Because those Taliban are here right now."

He squeezed the trigger and watched the man fall—revealing a second man just behind.

His M-4 spoke again, taking that man down. And the one behind him. And the one behind him...

***

21

"How many did you end up shooting before the drones got there?" Farrell asked as he poured a single-malt scotch later that evening.

"I didn't do a head count," Piper told him, quickly knocking it back. "Twenty-five, maybe thirty." He reached for the bottle. "If your little terminators had arrived a few minutes later…"

"They didn't, though." Farrell smiled. "You know I'm always going to be there for you."

"Yeah," Piper took another slug. "I know that."

"What's bothering you?"

"I haven't seen my family in a while," Piper shrugged. "There's been no time…" He looked at his friend. "Sean got into trouble—the FBI came to visit."

"What did he do?"

"Seems he got curious about his grades," Piper shook his head. "So he hacked into the school's mainframe to take a look and set off some kind of alarm…"

"That might be my fault." Farrell smiled sheepishly. "Hackers are going to be a really valuable commodity pretty soon—so I gave Sean a laptop for his Birthday gift—one that has a lot of Agency software loaded into it."

"He's only fourteen years old!"

"Young is the best time to learn." Farrell shook his head. "Hell, I can pilot a drone but it's a chore for me to program my TiVo! Real computer experts—men and women who can think in code and stay one step ahead of the hackers are the future of counterintelligence."

"So hackers are the next big threat?" Piper shook his head. "You've got some imagination!" He grinned. "Next thing you know, you'll tell me its pollution!"

"Don't laugh. Those guys——the ones out there," he gestured to the Afghan mountains visible through the O-Club windows. "Might be a problem right now but you know we're going to handle them when we get serious it. The guys with the computers, though. They're going to be the next big problem.

He looked at his friend. "The really serious enemy—the one who might be able to beat us—is the one who figures out how to get inside the machines we depend on for so much," another gesture, upwards this time. "Inside so he can control the satellites that handle our communications and orient our GPS systems. Get into the drones that we send into battle to save pilot's lives, take control of the systems that keep our Cruise missiles on course…" He looked Piper in the eye. "Negating any of those things would constitute a real threat."

"Science fiction!"

"Not at all." Farrell poured another drink. "One of these days, someone's going to figure out how to break into some important computerized system— maybe the electrical grid, maybe the banks." He looked at his friend. "That's when we're going to be forced to find new ways to fight back."

"I'll be long gone by then," Piper took another drink. "And you'll probably be the one responsible." He smiled at his friend. "If it works out that way, find a job for Sean." He grinned. "He'll probably be good at it."

***

"There're a lot of ragheads out there," Piper reported. "I don't think we have enough security to protect the subject if things go south."

"Not to worry," Farrell replied. "We've got more men out in the annex, and serious air support less than two hours away." There was a chuckle. "You've got everything you need to hold out for two hours, don't you?"

"I guess." Piper shrugged. "Although I'm surprised that you don't have drones ready to fly in and bust things up at a moment's notice."

"There are none in range." Farrell's voice was half-angry, half-joking. "We requested one or two to keep in orbit overhead but State said it would be 'provocative'."

"And State is never wrong."

"They do have one of their top people out there with you. I doubt they'd just throw him to the wolves."

"I don't know—remember what happened in Benghazi..." There was a long pause. "Hold one; they're getting a little noisy down there..."

Farrell glanced at the monitor that showed the various video feeds he had managed to get on line. The crowd outside the residence they'd chosen for the meeting was certainly growing larger—and he could see raised fists and yelling faces.

"We're starting to take some gunfire now," Piper reported as he came back on the line. "Just the odd potshot but..."

There was a loud crash followed by a long pause before: "That wasn't a rifle! I think..." Another pause. "Okay, they've got mortars out there—and they've already got them zeroed in on this place. I doubt we can hold out against that level of firepower..."

"Do what you can," Farrell picked up his secure telephone. "I'll get help moving."

"Roger that." Farrell heard Piper firing his rifle. "Don't take too long," Farrell heard more rifle fire chattering over the connection. "'Cause we don't have a lot of time ..."

There was an explosion just before the line went dead.

Farrell dialed a number on the secure phone and spoke quickly. "This is Farrell at site four-nine. We have activity at the Mission..."

"Roger four-nine, wait one..."

Farrell bit his lip as the line went quiet. On the surveillance screen, he could see more and more activity around the Mission. The crowd now numbered in the hundreds and he could see the flash of weapons coming from far too many places in that crowd.

"Site four-nine?" The voice that came from the phone was eerily calm. "This is Home Base."

"Roger Home Base."

"Say again situation?"

"Many—I say again, MANY unfriendlies attacking the residence—I can see rifle fire and my team inside the Mission reports incoming mortar rounds as well."

"They can't have mortars," the voice said. "They haven't had time to get them into position."

25

"My source is there, sir—inside the building." Farrell snarled. "If he says there are mortars, you can bet there are mortars."

"All right," there was a sigh. "I'll pass this on to higher headquarters and find out what they want us to do."

"Sir, we have men in harm's ways—under attack and at risk."

"Higher headquarters will decide what to do—is that clear?" The voice came back.

"Clear, sir."

"Good," another sigh. "Stand by your phone. I'll get back to you as soon as I can."

"Roger." Farrell kept a lid on his temper and did not slam the phone into its cradle as he wanted. Instead, he carefully lowered it as he watched the action in front of the Mission heat up.

Looks like there are a couple of hundred rioters out there, he thought. And Piper's got—what—four effectives? He glared at the phone. Higher headquarters better make up their minds pretty damn quick or I'll... Farrell hesitated. What could he do? He only had ten reliable fighters in the Annex. Even if he got all of them into the fight right now, what good could they do?

He stared at the screens, watching as the crowd surging around the Mission grew larger...

Come on, Piper! Hold on! Hold on just as long as you can...

***

Crap! Piper flinched as a mortar round hit the interior courtyard of the building the CIA had chosen for their meeting. A few more hits like that and the walls will come down!

26

He was scanning the crowd, looking for leaders, assessing threats. Most of the men he could see were just milling around, angered by something they had heard in the Mosque, but not willing to spill blood over it.

Others, however, the ones Piper was really searching for—were far more focused.

There's one, Piper put the aiming dot of his M-4 on the forehead of a man holding an AK-47 and haranguing a group near the left edge of the crowd.

He's herding the mob in our direction. Piper thought as he stroked the trigger, keeping his optics on the man long enough to watch the round impact just behind his target's left eye, caving in that side of his skull.

Okay, that's one down. He kept scanning, his gaze moving slowly from left to right. Who's my next customer…?

Another mortar round struck—this one deeper in the courtyard. Piper ducked down as bits of rock hit his back.

Wish we could reach that mortar; he straightened up and resumed his search for targets. If we could knock that out, we might stand a chance…

He saw a man near the center of the crowd hold his arms up and begin to scream in Arabic. That was enough to allow him to drop his sights onto the agitator's chest and softly squeeze the trigger…

There was a cry to his right. He swiveled to see that Blanchard had gone down. His absence left a chunk of wall free of cover--clear for rioters, some of whom were already climbing over...

They've gotten inside the compound, Piper realized. If they get to the gates and open them, the rest will come in. If that happens we're cooked! He came to a quick decision. I've got to stop them! He moved toward Blanchard's position as he flipped his M-4 to 'Automatic' and began hosing the interlopers.

One man dropped. Two. Three…

Piper's rifle went dry. He pressed the magazine release, pulled a new mag from an ammo pouch, and slid it into place an instant before Piper released the charging handle and opened fire once again …

"Farrell!" He yelled into the earbud pickup as he took another man down. "They've broken through our perimeter!"

Even as he spoke, more men came over the wall, all of them carrying automatic rifles of one sort or another.

"I need back-up now! I need it NOW!"

There was no reply.

"Farrell!"

Another mortar round impacted in the courtyard, sending shrapnel zipping through the little compound. Piper winced as a red-hot piece bit into his calf.

No time to worry about that now, he turned toward the men who were now coming over the wall in a steady stream. Got to clear them out…

He killed three, four, ten, a dozen…

"Farrell!" He saw Whitney go down. "Farrell! Where's the air cover! Where's…"

The courtyard was filled with rioters now--far too many for to stop with or without air cover.

Piper disengaged and began looking for a way out. If he could reach the main house—he might be able to fort up until help came. If it ever does!

He changed magazines and emptied the new one into the crowd, then smashed the nearest attacker in the face with the rifle butt and drew his pistol...

***

"Crap!" Farrell cursed as he saw Piper go down—overwhelmed by the sheer number of attackers.

Others were already smashing their way into the residence.

He picked up the phone and gnashed his teeth as he waited for headquarters to answer...

"This is Farrell," he spoke as soon as 'Home Base' answered. "Where's my back-up!"

"Higher Headquarters has ordered all units to stand down." The answer came.

"Stand down?!" Farrell stared at the phone. "My people are dying! The subject..."

"Your orders are to stand down—do you understand?"

"No," Farrell snarled. "I do not understand."

"Agent Farrell—you will stand down. This is an order."

"Shove your damn order up your ass! I'm not going to let those men die..."

"There's nothing you can do Farrell. You have no back-up, no air cover." The voice on the other end of the line hesitated. "Deal with it."

"Deal with it?" Farrell shook his head. "That's all you're going to say?"

"That is all I am at liberty to say."

"Well screw you!" Farrell yelled into the mouthpiece. "And screw whoever came up with this damned decision."

"Farrell!"

"What are you going to do?" Farrell sneered. "Are you going to fire me?" He shook his head. "Too late for that!" He was holding the phone at arm's length now, shouting into the mouthpiece. "I quit!"

He slammed the phone down into the cradle, cracking the hard plastic with the force of his rage.

CHAPTER ONE

NEW YORK CITY

"What do you think, Marty? Do you have time to join me at Dominic's?" Jason gave his friend a weak smile. "You could keep me from getting drunk and making a fool of myself with Megan."

The Megan his friend didn't want to make a fool of himself in front of was, Marty Alarnick knew, was the good-looking redhead that had recently started work at Dominic's Bar.

"Why don't you just ask her out and get it over with?"

"Can't," Jason shook his head. "Pretty girls intimidate me." He grinned. "That's why I drink!"

"And you expect me to stop you?"

"No," another shake of the head. "I expect you to slow me down a little."

"Okay," Marty shrugged. "I've got nothing else going." He patted his wallet. "Gotta stop at an ATM first, though."

"No problem," Jason gestured toward the elevator. "There's a Chase bank on the way."

The bank in question was actually quite close. Marty pushed his card into the slot and touched the 'GET CASH' indicator then the $60 button—he couldn't afford to spend more than that.

The machine whirred and clicked for a long moment before a wad of bills was pushed out of the cash slot at the bottom.

A very thick wad of bills. So thick that twenty-dollar bills began to be ejected from the center of the wad out onto the floor.

"Hey!" Marty reached for the overflowing wad as he yelled for his companion. "Look at this!"

"Wow!" Jason looked at the bills on the floor and the pile in Marty's hand. "There must be four or five hundred dollars there!"

"I only asked for $60."

"Try it again," Jason grinned. "Who knows, maybe it'll give you another wad of cash!"

"Yeah," Marty once again fed his card into the machine. "I guess it's worth a try..."

***

Far to the South, slender hands flew deftly across a keyboard...

"I think that takes care of the Professor's needs," the owner of the hands, one Sarah Lawrence, muttered to herself. "Now it's time to take my share..."

"You see, Professor?" The voice came from a point almost directly behind her. "I told you she couldn't be trusted."

Sarah whirled to find Jayson—a tall, chocolate-skinned young man pointing at her screen. Next to him was an older, shorter man.

"I told you not to risk taking extra cash, did I not?" Professor Ramnarain was a wiry, olive-skinned man of about forty. "There is, after all, no need for it."

"Professor, I..."

"You know why I asked you to hack the ATM system. We discussed it at some length." The Professor moved a step closer. "We gave you the job because you had experience—you assured us that you had done such things several times before."

"I did..." Sarah spread her hands in supplication. "It's why I'm sure there's no way to trace the money I shifted to our accounts..."

"Our accounts?" Jayson sneered. "With an 'S'? I thought you were given the task of moving the funds we need for our operation to the account the Professor gave you. One that cannot be accessed by anyone except us."

"Anyone except him!" She spat back. "I don't mind stealing what cash the team needs—but I'm damned sure going to take the opportunity to fatten my own account." She sneered into the tall young man's face. "Do you have a problem with that?"

Jayson started to answer, but before he could shape the words, another, female, voice came from behind them. "It appears you were correct, Jayson." An older woman, spare and hard-looking moved closer to the group around the computer. "She cannot be trusted." The woman produced a hunting knife. "Please take care of her for us?"

The slim young man accepted the knife and nodded, taking a long step toward the suddenly frightened young woman."

"We're going to need another hacker," the woman noted, ignoring the muffled sounds behind her.

"I'll have to find someone," the Professor turned away and began walking out of the computer room. "I have a program that will cast a net and tell us if there's anyone within, what, three hundred miles?"

"Make it five hundred," the woman replied. "That'll bring New York into play."

"Five hundred miles." The Professor nodded. "I'll set it to find anyone within five hundred miles with the kind of hacking skills we need—we can pick and choose from whatever comes up."

CHAPTER TWO

WASHINGTON HEIGHTS, NY

Sean Piper smiled as his fingers flew over the keyboard of his laptop. *This is going to be easy!* He glanced over his shoulder at Angie, a good-looking young blonde who was watching his every move. *I could get in there now, but...*

"I'm sorry, Angie." Sean lifted his hands from the keyboard. "It looks as if I can't hack the password for the Chem Department."

Angie Kurtz was slim, blond, and, to Sean's eyes, extremely hot. She was close enough to give him goosebumps, and when she touched him...

He smiled, thinking of the extra time he spent in the shower most mornings.

Angie was perfectly aware of all (well, most) of that—she had long known the power her looks gave her—and more had long since learned the easiest way to use that power to get what she wanted.

It had helped her keep her parents happy by staying near the top of her class in High School. When she ran into a problem—like an upcoming test she hadn't properly prepared for—she just found a boy to coach her through it or, in extreme cases, she could usually find a teacher who was perfectly willing—eager in many cases—to give her what she wanted in exchange for a little of this or a little of that...

Now, in her first year of college, she had discovered that things weren't quite as easy. To succeed, she would need some very specialized help.

The kind of help Sean Piper could give her.

"I thought you were doing well in Chem 101."

"I was for a while," Angie shook her head. "But I missed a couple of classes and..." She shrugged—in High School it had been easy to get a teacher to help with missed work—or, in many cases, just fix her grade to appear that she had done the work.

That was then.

Now she had to deal with Mr. Knox—the professor who taught Chem 101. Mr. Knox was very straightforwardly gay—and quite immune to her charms.

Forcing her to depend on Sean.

"So," she moved closer, ran a hand down his arm. "Can you help me?"

Sean shivered a little at her touch. "Maybe..." He shook his head. "But I can't get in tonight." He turned toward her, looked her in the eye (which was a chore for him at the moment—there were so many other things to look at...)

I'll need some time to work out a new entry point." He forced his gaze to Angie's light blue eyes. "Can we get together tomorrow night—I should have something then."

"Sure," she brushed his lips with a light kiss. "I'll look forward to it." She stood up, heading for the door. "Say, eight o'clock or so?"

Sean swallowed twice before answering. "Eight will be fine—I'll do a little work overnight and, hopefully, have something that'll work tomorrow."

"Good," she stopped by the door and turned toward him and smiled, leaning just far enough forward that her bra-less breasts pushed against her t-shirt. "I'll be waiting."

Sean packed his laptop and stood up, letting the shoulder bag hang down in front of him so she couldn't see just how much that little view had done to him. "Tomorrow night." He tried for another kiss, got only her cheek. "See you then."

The door closed behind him.

She really is a bit of a pricktease, he thought as he headed down the stairs. Still, he smiled. She's very nice to look at!

***

Sean kept thinking about Angie as he walked home. With his Dad moving from base to base, Sean had gone from school to school on a regular basis. His grades didn't suffer—he'd been born with a sharp mind and a near-photographic memory, the combination gave him an advantage over the other kids that made up for the changes in schools.

But not his social life...

By the time he started at a new school, the kids had already formed into various cliques—and most of the girls had paired up with boys they'd grown up with. Sean always ended up the odd-man-out.

Over the years he'd labored to find a way around the 'new-kid' stigma. He had tried sports—he should have been a sensation with his tall and muscular build and quick reflexes-but most High School coaches had worked with the same youngsters for years and just didn't want to invest the time it would take to get a new kid—one that might move at any second--into the fold.

Sean tried simpler things—he joined the debate team for a while, then switched to the Drama Club. He found that while he had the looks to get on the stage, he lacked both the talent and drive it would take to make it worthwhile.

Eventually he gave up and accepted his lot in life, after all, he had other interests—books, his computer, his sister...

Every now and then he'd have to deal with a bully. It was no real problem for him, a young man who'd had years of training in various fighting skills. His father had insisted upon teaching Sean everything he knew, then, when he was satisfied, got some other Special Forces troops to come in and show Sean a bunch of new tricks.

That meant that on those rare occasions when some 'tough' classmate tried to force him to do something he didn't want to do; Sean was able to quickly and efficiently show him (and his cronies) the error of their ways.

He didn't cripple or kill anyone, although he could quite easily have done so—something he made quite clear to the beaten bully and his associates. After that one try, they left Sean completely alone.

Sean was happy enough—right up until fate dropped the hammer on him.

Twice.

First, his little sister was diagnosed with a serious Kidney problem—one that would require multiple surgeries to make right.

Then, just as his mom began to make plans for those surgeries, they got the word that his father was dead--killed during some kind of special mission in the Middle East (Sean and his mother weren't told more than that—it was 'classified').

From that day forward, Sean didn't care if he had friends or not. He was happy to be a loner, happy to spend his time on his studies and doing whatever he could to help his mother and sister.

And he spent a lot of time on the computer.

That computer--a quite advanced laptop—came as a gift from his Uncle Fred—one of his father's closest friends.

The computer was stuffed with games and graphics equipment and was protected by a very sturdy, military-grade case.

Uncle Fred told him that he had access to almost every game and website—and there were some very special programs that would help him if he ever needed access to something new—programs that Sean would have to teach himself how to use.

Use very sparingly.

Those programs sat untouched for more than a year as Seam explored the internet and found an escape from his unhappy school life in various games.

Eventually, though, he became curious about those 'special' programs and began to experiment.

He found that with their help he could do things that, he learned from chats with schoolmates and online friends, other computers could not do.

He began to explore more deeply and, after a great deal of practice, accidentally became an expert hacker.

When his mother was denied a military pension due to some kind of technicality that was never made clear, Sean used his newfound abilities to try to find out just what had happened to his father, thinking that information might help his mother fight for the money they needed so badly. But even with his special programs, he was blocked in every attempt—unable to hack into US Military codes or firewalls. It almost seemed as if the computer had been pre-programmed not to work in certain areas.

Mom, having already given up hope in any fight with the government, found a job that would pay just enough to put a roof over their heads and leave enough for her daughter's medical expenses.

A job that required them to move to New York City.

Sean shrugged when she told him. It was just another move—one of many—and another new school—just one more in a long line...

He was wrong about that. Sean had just graduated High School and found himself a college freshman. New—just like every other first-year student!

Some of his classmates did know one another from the old neighborhood or a shared High School, but most had come from different places around the State and were, like him, in a brand new environment.

For the first time in his life, he found himself starting out on a more or less even basis with everyone else.

In fact, he might be a little more than even.

At eighteen years of age, Sean was nearly full-grown. He stood a shade over six foot three—a height that his mother, tired of buying new clothes for her sprouting son, hoped would stick.

His last growth spurt had left him lean and mean, his baby fat gone along with the worst of his acne.

He was a good-looking young man—and, with a new opportunity to succeed, he threw himself into the college's social world...

His first success came when he found his first real girlfriend--Angie. Sean had noticed the pretty blonde during freshman orientation—as had every other hetero young man in the group. How could they help themselves? Angie was a striking young woman--tall and well-built in a willowy sort of way, Angie sported long, naturally blonde hair, fully-developed breasts, and baby blue eyes that seemed oh-so-innocent.

Sean had dreams about her—odd dreams--and wondered if he should even dare to ask her out.

But he had no money—something he knew he would need with someone like Angie, so he hesitated...

And found a way to solve the money problem. His skills with the computer had reached a point where he could effortlessly crack the school's firewalls, allowing him access to every department's libraries...

Which held all their tests. With the answers.

It wasn't something he needed to maintain his own grades—he was doing quite well without the help.

But there were others who were having problems and they were more than happy to quietly purchase the questions for an upcoming test (Sean never sold answers).

Although he was making quite a bit more money than he expected, Sean was kind of uneasy about what he was doing. He knew that his mother would never approve—so he salved his conscience by giving her most of what he made to put toward his sister's medical expenses, keeping only a small percentage of his income for his own purposes and promising himself that when he had enough, he would ask Angie out on a date. Dinner and a film perhaps...

It would be a start.

Then, one afternoon, she approached him...

"Hey," he felt the hairs on his arm stand up as she stopped in front of him. "Want to hang out?" She smiled as he stared at her, speechless. "Relax, I don't bite!" Her smile widened, showing even white teeth. "At least not on a first date..."

And she didn't—but she did lay her golden head on his shoulder as they watched a film on TV while snuggling close enough to allow him to feel the firm young flesh under her t-shirt...

For Sean, it was a fantasy come true. He wasn't stupid—he knew she had ulterior motives-- but at the moment he didn't care. Hell, if she was going to use him, he was more than justified in using her!

Now, halfway through the semester, she wanted—needed—his help really badly...

And Sean was ready to give it for her—as leverage for some of the things he wanted...

Mom wouldn't approve of what I have in mind, he realized. Neither would Dad. He bit his lip. I'll have to think about it...

He was still sorting it out when he reached the little apartment he shared with his mother and sister...

CHAPTER THREE

AIR TRAFFIC CONTROL CENTER, NORTH EAST SECTOR ISLIP, NY

"United one six Heavy, turn right to three one zero and increase altitude to one five angels." Eric Moore nodded to himself as he watched the airliner turn onto the newly-specified path and moved the marker for that flight off his rack. That one belongs to the Canadians now... He leaned back for a quick breather—and shook his head in disgust as his right hand automatically twitched toward his shirt pocket.

Amazing! It's more than five years now but I still have the urge to grab a cigarette when I take even a short break! He glanced at the screen, rubbing his chin as he automatically searched for any new symbols joining the traffic pattern.

It was a good idea for the FAA to ban smoking in the center... He leaned back in his chair and looked up. But it would also have been a good idea to spend a couple of bucks to overhaul this place after they put the ban in place! He stared at the brownish-yellow stains that covered the white ceiling tiles. There's enough leftover smoke-stench trapped in the chairs, rug, and ceiling of this dump to keep all of us on a nicotine high right up until the day we retire!

He stretched his neck, trying—in vain--to alleviate the nearly permanent kink there. At least, he thought. It's a quiet night--not too much traffic. He looked around at the other controllers. Maybe it's even quiet enough for me to get a start on the shift's paperwork!

Before that thought went any further, he saw his radar screen flicker and go completely dark before, almost instantaneously, flashing back to normal illumination.

"What the hell!" Eric looked at the other controllers. "Anyone else see that?"

He got a positive response. Everyone had seen what he had.

"I wonder what the hell happened." Eric leaned forward to stare at his screen. "It can't just drop out and go dead—we have all kinds of backups..." His eyes caught the marker for the United flight he had just handed off—it was in the wrong place!

She's off course by nearly fifteen degrees! He realized, staring in shocked disbelief.

How is that possible?

He turned his full attention to the screen, checking the computer-generated markers against the handwritten ones on his backup grid, comparing what should be actual aircraft positions to those flashing on his board.

That AirTran heavy... He stared at the transceiver signal—the plane was nearly twenty degrees off course—and low—far too low.

Really worried now, he checked the next signal. A Jet Blue commuter flight... He shook his head. This one's too high!

"Damn!" Eric sat straight up in his chair and felt his dinner curdle in his stomach as he realized what was happening. Every single plane on my screen is off course in one way or another! That can only mean...

He stood up, straightening his back as he looked at the hunched backs of the other three controllers on duty.

"Everybody!" He made sure his voice did not reveal the panic inside. "Listen up!" They turned to look at him, eyes a bit glassy after nearly a full shift of staring at their screens. "The computer information you're seeing on the screens is wrong!" He bent down to the master console that sat next to his screen and flipped the plastic safety cover off a button he had never before touched. "I'd hoped I'd never have to do this, but..." He pushed the button with one determined move, not giving himself time to give it too much thought.

Aircraft markers disappeared from every screen in the center, replaced by raw radar data.

"We're on manual as of now!" He looked at the shocked faces of the others. "I said go on manual! Get everyone up there on the merry-go-round until we can put them back on course!"

The controllers kept staring.

"Do it, God damn it!"

Eric stood there glaring at the stunned group until they finally got the message and turned back to their screens to begin the laborious task of matching the information on their back-up racks with the ill-defined target smears on the screen.

It took a while but one by one, they identified their responsibilities and began to work the radios: "American two three, maintain altitude and orbit at present speed." "Continental three nine, orbit at one zero angels until further communication."

Okay. Eric took a few minutes to contact the planes on his own board, ordering them to circle until ordered otherwise. When he was sure they were complying, he passed those flights to the controller on his right. "I think that's got it under control for now," he told the other man. "Call me if anything changes."

When the man nodded, Eric stood and moved to the little office that overlooked the main control room—the office he seldom had time to use.

Pristine end-of-shift paperwork sat neatly stacked in the center of his desk, waiting for him to fill it out.

He pushed them to one side, grimacing. There's goanna be a hell of a lot more paperwork to deal with before I go home tonight!

He took a seat and picked up institutional black phone that sat on the edge of his desk. The thing was huge, made of heavy plastic with an ancient rotary dial--which showed just how long it had been since it had been used. He started to dial his boss's number—then stopped and thought about what had to be done before this was all over with.

It might be better if I start off by kicking this further up the ladder. He nodded at the thought. It's possible we're not the only center that was affected and even if we are, the big shots are going to get into it sooner or later. He nodded once. In this case, sooner will be a whole lot better for everyone concerned—most especially me! He put the black phone down and laid a shaking hand on the red phone that sat next to it at the very edge of his desk. He'd never touched the red phone before—not even in drills.

He snapped the seal and picked up the headset, then placed his right forefinger on the single white button set in the middle of the phone's face—and pushed.

There was no ring or tone of any kind, just a long moment of silence before a no-nonsense, utterly professional sort of voice answered—one that seemed neither male nor female awhile displaying not a hint of feeling. "Yes?"

"This is the North-East Center." Eric was surprised to find his own voice sounded equally firm and professional. "We've got a problem—I think it could have originated from outside..."

"Is it under control?" He heard a touch of concern now—but no panic.

"For the moment." Eric took a deep breath. "I switched the computers off as soon as I saw what was happening—this center is now running on manual protocols. We can maintain the load for a while—maybe a couple of hours if we have to."

"Good." The voice was calm. "Your name?"

"Eric Moore". Another deep breath. "Second-shift supervisor."

"Thank you Mr. Moore. Please make sure no one leaves the center. We'll have a team there in 30 minutes or less."

"Thirty minutes." Eric watched the controllers as they shifted the tiles in their rack, carefully maintaining order in the skies over New York and the surrounding area. "Yeah, we can hold it together for that long..." He touched his pocket. I could really use a cigarette now! He told himself ruefully. Rules or no rules...

***

"That didn't work, Professor." The young black man shook his head as he watched the data on

48

his screen. "They went manual before anything much happened."

"That doesn't matter—we didn't really care about the result of our little experiment," the older man's tone was even and measured—another lecture by the 'Professor'. "It will suffice to show them that we can access their traffic control system—they will look for ways to stop us from doing so in future."

"So we ask for the money now?" A female voice—young, slightly nervous, asked.

"Not yet." The Professor shook his head. "I think we'll give them one more demonstration first." He turned to the young man. "Do we have something prepared?"

"I think so," the young man nodded. "Mr. Mize was working on a series of programs..."

"They're ready," the youngster identified as 'Mize' spoke up. "We can put them into action whenever you like."

"Good," the Professor smiled. "Let us activate them tomorrow morning." He gestured. "Early tomorrow morning—around rush hour..."

***

NEW YORK TRANSIT AUTHORITY CONTROL
CHAMBERS STREET, NY

Like the FAA, the NYTA had banned smoking at its various headquarters in the mid-nineties. From the day that ban had gone into effect, Transit Authority workers had ignored it, continuing to smoke what they liked and where they liked—just as they always had--secure in the sure and certain knowledge that their union was far too powerful for the city to take on over so trivial an infraction.

"Ready to roll 'em out?" Willie Sovino chewed on an unlit cigar as he scanned the brightly-lit controls spread out before him. The whole board had gone dark several minutes earlier—he would never have noticed had he not just taken his seat. It had reset itself almost instantly, lighting up before he even had time to get a good round or cursing in.

Piece of shit, he thought. I'll have maintenance in to look it over as soon as the first rush is over.

He didn't really have a lot of faith in the computers they were using anyway—the old way, to Willie's mind, was still the best.

"Looks good from here." Arlen Miller had been with the NYTA for nearly 15 years. He'd worked his way up from a lowly track worker to a supervisory position, finally landing his very important present spot as the assistant operations manager.

This, the very first hour of the shift, when fresh rolling stock had to be moved from holding areas onto the mainline, was his least favorite time of the day. I still get nightmares about what would happen if all those extra trains rolled onto the mainline at the wrong time. He grinned to himself. It's stupid, I know. It just can't happen with all the safeguards we have in place, but if it did happen…

He glanced at the telltales on his screen. "Okay, Willie. Looks good here. Let 'em loose!"

Sovino, from his own position a few feet away, took one last look at his own board before nodding and touching the necessary controls on his panel. "Okay—I've released the cars from the Rockaway yard—they'll roll onto the Eastern Parkway and Jamaica lines…" His brow furrowed as he glanced up at the video screens set at the very top of his console. "Hey—you sure it's clear in the city?"

Arlen checked the telltales again. "Everything's green…"

"Look at the monitors!" Willie's hands moved quickly. "Somethin's not right!"

His assistant glanced at the bank of TV screens in front of the twin consoles. I don't see… Then he caught a glimpse of movement that shouldn't be there. Oh God! He glanced back at his console—all the lights were still green. "I don't understand…"

"No time to figure it out now!" Willie was popping the plastic cover on the emergency override. "Get ready to shut it down—quick!"

Miller's eyes locked on the TV. He couldn't tear them away as the B train ran straight through Canal Street station—never even slowing down as it hurtled uptown where three trains already loaded with early morning commuters were stacked up.

We're not going to be able to stop them! Miller thought as he scanned all of the screens, each of which showed more empty trains coming from the yards and speeding through stations or other checkpoints as they moved toward midtown…

JC's down there. Arlen' brain raced as he tried to remember his son's work schedule. I think he said that he had to be at 1 Penn Central by 7AM…

"Arlen!" Willie's voice was frantic now. "Snap out of it!"

Miller tore his eyes away from the monitors and quickly snapped the safety cover off his own shutdown. "Okay Willie, I'm okay. It was just…"

"Understood." Sovino had spent his whole career on these controls and ones like them. He was just about ready to put in his papers and retire. Just my luck, he thought, watching the hurtling trains on the monitor screens. They'll probably try to say this is my fault and cancel my pension! He glanced over at his co-worker. "Okay Arlen, on my count…" He held his thumb over the red button of the emergency shut-down. "Three…" He saw his friend's finger move into position. Both buttons had to be pushed at the same time or the system would not shut down. "Two…" He glanced at the screen. The B train would reach 34th in another minute or so. "Now!" He punched down on the red button just as Miller did the same on his twinned console. That oughta do it…

The room went dark as main power cut off. Willie sighed and pulled out his lighter. All we can do now is wait.

CHAPTER FOUR

J. EDGAR HOOVER BUILDING, WASHINGTON D.C.

"How many did we lose?" Martin Lawrence Seward was only thirty-five years old. He looked sixty-five--three years as the National Security Council's counter-terrorism chief could do that to a man—and he already knew that this morning's meeting wasn't going to make him feel any younger.

"It wasn't as bad as it could have been." Mary Max Halston was several decades younger than her boss, but the strain of the job had already added years to her once-pretty face. "The Air Traffic Control problem was contained almost immediately—the night supervisor was working a console and saw the intrusion and its result almost as it happened." She closed the cover on the report in front of her. "He had the sense to immediately pull the mainframe offline and go to manual operation. If he had hesitated or taken the time to call his superiors instead of acting…" Her shrug was eloquent.

"It's a good thing the FAA has enough budget problems that it hasn't been able to fully automate its centers, Seward put in. "And it's even better that they were lucky enough to have a supervisor with the brains to recognize a problem when he saw it." He saw the quick nods of agreement around the table and motioned for Mary Max to continue. "What happened with the NY Subway system?"

"That was, in its way, trickier," Mary Max touched a button on the control panel set into the table in front of her. A screen descended from the wall opposite the table, and a diagram was already glowing on its surface. "You'll note the red and green-marked lines."

There was a general mutter of agreement around the table.

"The red ones are the main arteries used for the morning rush, the green ones feed new rolling stock onto the mains just before that rush starts." She touched a button and several new amber lines superimposed themselves onto the red. "The amber indicates the points where yellow caution signals and automated spacing go into play to insure that newly arrived stock does not roll onto an active track." She looked around the table. "It's a solid piece of design."

She touched another button and an enhanced TV picture appeared as an inset at the bottom right corner of the screen. "Theoretically, the computer control system makes it impossible for new trains to enter a line while existing cars are within 100 yards of the switch position—that is an automatic constraint that is supposed to be backed up by a series of traffic lights that tell the engineer of each train that the line in front of him is clear."

She indicated the TV picture. "This is the backup tape from the camera that covers the Chambers to Canal Street segment of the tunnels, You will note that new trains are entering the main track less than a half mile ahead." She enlarged the

54

picture until the traffic signal to the right of the tunnel filled the entire screen.

"That light is green!"

"That's right sir." She used a laser pointer to indicate two more visible traffic lights. "If you'll look further, you will note that every signal in sight is green." She touched the controls again, bringing up a different recording of a different monitor screen. "This is the Canal to 14th Street area."

"All those are green as well!"

Another switch of picture. "This is 14th to 23rd Street."

"Green!"

"23rd to 28th"

"All right." Seward rubbed his eyes. "How far did this go?"

"As far as we can tell," Mary Max cleared the screen, put up a map of the entire subway system. "Every indicator in the system went to green at precisely 05:49."

"That's not possible!" Willie Granelli and Arlen Miller had been rushed to McLean immediately after the incident so that they could be available for this meeting. Now, as the elder manager stared at the image on the screen, his voice didn't waver. "We checked every control before we began moving stock onto the mainline. All the indicators checked out just fine!"

"According to your board." Mary Max leaned toward the two men. "And your board runs off the same computer system as these lights, does it not?"

"Well, yeah…"

"Gentlemen, please know that we do not blame you in any way for what almost happened." Seward

55

waved a hand in the air. "On the contrary, your quick action saved many lives."

"Then just why are we here?" Arlen Miller snarled. He'd been desperately trying to reach a phone since before he left New York. He needed to know if his son was all right but had not been able to contact him. He didn't carry a cell phone—they were useless inside the OP center which was underground and surrounded by pipes and wires, and he hadn't had the time to reach an outside phone before the Feds appeared in response to their SOS. Since then he had not been allowed to make any calls at all.

"I haven't been allowed to call my wife and tell her where I am—and my son…"

"Your son was on the double-A train from Chambers to 42nd Street when the incident started." Mary Max's face was stony as she studied the open report in front of her. "It was one of three trains that were too close to the oncoming stock to stop when you gentlemen turned the power off."

"Was it…" Miller was almost afraid to ask the question. "Was it hit?"

"The double-A was crushed between three other trains." Mary Max's eyes moistened even while she kept her face stony and unmoving. "Three hundred fifteen people were killed or injured."

"My son?"

"Is in Mount Sinai Medical Center." She caught Miller's eyes and held them. "He is expected to recover."

"Thank God!" The big supervisor let his face fall into his hands as Granelli, his partner and friend, put an arm over his shoulder. "Thank God."

56

Mary Max turned her attention back to the other men and women around the long table. "In the entire system, at least five hundred people were killed and another thousand to fifteen hundred have injuries of varying severity."

"Two thousand men, women, and children!" Seward's voice was low.

"At last count." Mary Max put a new table up on the screen. "We were lucky—it could easily have been far worse." Her pointer indicated the number of people who would have been in the subway system just fifteen minutes later. "If they had made their move just a little later..." She pointed at the huddled forms of Miller and Granelli. "Or if these men hadn't been as alert—and hadn't reacted as quickly as they did..." She shook her head. "Casualties could easily have been in the tens of thousands."

"Do we know who was responsible for this?" Seward turned toward a man at the far end of the table.

"It's too soon to say." Frank Farrell glanced at his notes. "I can tell you with some certainty that the worm—it was a worm, by the way—was inserted into the New York area transportation control systems through their internet connection." He looked up. "Our Initial investigation seems to indicate that they came from a server and IP address somewhere outside the Continental US."

"Seems to indicate?" The questioner wore the uniform of a Colonel in the US Army.

"We found a partial IP address in the ATC worm—when Mr. Moore shut the system down, he stopped the worm from finishing its work and self-destructing. We were able to do a complete dump of the system and that gave us enough bits and pieces to partially reconstruct the artefact." Farrell indicated a page of coding that appeared on the screen. "Note the address…"

"You're kidding, I trust." Seward leaned forward. "I can't even set the time on my DVR and you expect me to read that!"

"Sorry, sir." Farrell touched a control and most of the coding disappeared, leaving a short series of numbers. "This is the address, and it indicates that the worm was downloaded somewhere within the Indian subcontinent."

"Where two thirds of the world's coding is done." Mary Max shook her head. "That's not much help."

"Perhaps not." Farrell gestured. "But it does tell us that this was a deliberate attack from an outside source, not some virus generated by a pimple-faced hacker in Newark!"

"That is something, I suppose." Seward stroked his chin. "All right, I think I've heard enough for the moment." He stood and stepped toward Granelli and Miller, putting a hand on the grieving man's arm. "Gentlemen, I give you my sincerest thanks." He helped them to their feet before solemnly shaking each of their hands. "Without your quick action, we would have many additional casualties to grieve over." He motioned to the Army Officer. "Colonel Martini will personally see to it that you are taken to the hospital as quickly as possible, Mr. Miller—and we will make it clear to the authorities there that they are handling a very special case." He smiled at Miller's grateful look. "It's the least we can do."

Seward returned to his chair as the military man led the two civilians out of the room, he shook his head bemusedly as he saw Granelli pull a cigar out of his pocket and bite into the end. Then he turned back to the others: "All right Ladies and Gentlemen," he drummed his fingers on the table in front of him. "Now that we're certain we've been hit by foreign action, what are we going to do about it?"

"I thought we had firewalls in place at all critical computer interfaces." Jamison looked at Farrell. "Wasn't that part of your portfolio, Frank?"

The ex-CIA man shrugged. "We have installed the best firewalls available." He looked around the table. "Apparently, they weren't good enough." He shook his head. "As I've said many times, no passive system will ever be powerful enough to guard all our critical interfaces—there are too many avenues of access."

"We have to do something!" Seward's face was clouding over. "We can't allow this sort of thing to happen again! What if the next time, nobody catches it until it's too late?"

"Well, sir." Farrell turned to the head of the table. "I think the best thing we can do right now is find who is responsible for this incident and make them pay." He looked Seward in the face. "Not just put them in jail for a couple of years—make them pay in a more permanent fashion," his face went hard. "It would serve as a deterrent against others who might contemplate the same action."

"And how do you plan to do that? I mean, the current administration wants to close Gitmo! Do you think they'd allow you to just execute a bunch of hackers?"

Farrell smiled and shrugged. "Well sir, the administration doesn't have to know about everything we do—does it?

CHAPTER FIVE

J. EDGAR HOOVER BUILDING--
WASHINGTON D.C.

"That attack didn't come from India," Farrell told Mary Max over two vending machine sandwiches a few hours later. "Whoever did it just bounced it through a series of servers. That meant that the final address was, quite by chance, in Mumbai."

"Do you have an idea where it did come from?"

"I'm working on that." Farrell looked at his boss. "First indications tell me that it came from somewhere inside the United States."

"What," Mary Max picked up the second half of her rather dry ham sandwich and studied it for a long moment. "What makes you think that?"

"The target." Farrell's sandwich was long gone. He took a sip of his coffee—the only thing left in front of him. "Whoever did this wasn't looking for data—they were solely interested in creating havoc and destruction—the kind that would scare people." He shook his head. "That suggests they're looking for a payoff of some kind."

"Blackmail? Protection?"

"Either would fit." Farrell took another drink. "The attacks couldn't have done that much damage on their own—even if all the supervisors had been sound asleep! At worst they wouldn't have affected more than a few thousand people—but that many deaths would have frightened the whole country—

and made them think something even bigger might be coming. That level of fear would force our current leadership to pay up without even thinking about it." He grinned wryly, "Remember those sailors off the coast of Iran."

"Okay, I'll buy that." Mary Max put her sandwich down and reached for her own coffee cup. "So where's the ransom demand?"

"I think they'll go for another demonstration before they send one," Farrell's mouth was set in a grim line. "They didn't get much publicity on this one—all the media stories stressed the 'heroic action' of the supervisors at both sites." He shook his head. "That's not going to suit our would-be terrorists at all."

"So what do we do?"

"We check on all the firewalls we have—and make sure that everyone liable to be in jeopardy is alert to the possibility of an attack." He drained his mug and looked her in the eye. "And I'd like to recruit Sean Piper to help. He might be able to infiltrate the group."

"Who is Sean Piper?" Mary Max dropped the partially-eaten sandwich back onto her plate and stared at it balefully.

"I'm sure I told you about him. He's the son of Robert Piper—one of my assets in the sandbox."

"Frank! That makes him, what, eighteen years old? We don't have time to run him through the farm..."

"We don't need to do that kind of training with him. His Dad's been training the kid since he was five. He's got more physical skill then anyone I know--and he's smart." Frank smiled. "And that computer we gave him has really paid off—he's really slick with it." He looked at his boss. "He can be a real help."

"I remember him now." Mary Max raised an eyebrow. "He almost got into the Pentagon Records Office with that computer you gave him."

"Yeah, he was looking for his Dad's packet." Farrell glared at Mary Max. "You know they denied his mother's request for a pension, right?"

"I do now." Mary Max made a note. "I'll see what can be done about that." She looked at Farrell. "You're sure the kid can help?"

"I think there's a pretty good chance the kid can get inside—and if he does, he can lead us right to them!"

"Why makes you think they'll try to recruit him?"

Farrell pulled out a finger drive and pushed it into the desk computer. "This is professor Ramnarain—he used to work for us." He looked at Mary Max. "He was our top computer guy for a long while."

"So?"

"He disappeared several months ago—along with two of his best students. Since then..." He pulled up a series of photographs. "A number of other young computer hackers we were keeping an eye on have gone missing. One of them," he stopped on the image of a young girl. "Sarah Lawrence was found knifed to death in the Potomac yesterday." He looked at her. "I think that Ramnarain is behind this—and I also think he's using these kids to do the actual hacking." He grinned thinly. "And right now, he's got an opening."

"Kind of cold-blooded on your part—I thought the kid's father was your friend!"

Farrell shrugged. "His father asked me to take care of Sean—find him a job." He looked at his boss. "This is the perfect way for him to start."

"Okay." Mary Max nodded. ""I'll take care of the various bulletins and warnings you want to put out." She picked up her own coffee mug. "You go see if the kid will play." She took a sip, grimaced. "Keep me posted."

"Yes, Ma'am." He nodded and stood up. "I will do just that."

"Make sure your phone is with you and on at all times! I don't want you to 'forget' and go off on your own!"

"I would never do a thing like that!" Farrell smiled. "I'll check in every couple of hours—I think we have a day or two before they try something else."

"A day!"

"That should give you enough time to get everyone up to speed."

"Yeah," Mary Max shook her head. "For whatever good that will do."

CHAPTER SIX

"So I worked out this gaming interface to allow us to get a better look at the school's firewall..."

Angie leaned in very close, the firm flesh of her left breast brushing against his arm as she did so. "Will it help us get in?" She turned toward him, sliding a little closer.

His pulse speeded up.

"I hope so." He nodded. "We just have to be careful not to set off any of the alarms. They might call in the FBI's Cyber guys to investigate if we do..."

"God!" Angie's brow puckered prettily at the thought. "My Dad would kill me if the FBI showed up here!"

"My Mom would be pretty upset too—she was certainly pissed off the last time I got nailed—and that was for some really penny-ante stuff!" Sean was leaning forward now, moving the joystick he was using to utilize his makeshift interface incrementally, carefully, as he allowed his avatar to drift across the face of the net that represented the Chemistry Department's firewall.

"Right now we just want to along slowly until we find a weak spot. Then we sneak through the firewall and get what we want."

The avatar inched along the face of the net. "When cyber-nerds build firewalls like this, they invariably make mistakes—they work long hours and when they get tired..." He pushed the joystick a hair more to one side. "They miss things—leave faults in the coding—faults that lead to gaps in coverage." He nodded once and smiled. "Like that one!"

The girl leaned in, eyes wide. But she couldn't see anything different...

"I don't see anything..."

"There's a gap..." He pointed at a tiny spot on the screen. "Right there." Sean nodded. "It might be big enough. I'll just get us through..."

"Could I try it?" Her blue eyes gazed into his entreatingly. "I'm pretty good with a joystick..."

"You've got to be real careful..." He passed the joystick to the girl's side of the table. "The controls work just like any game console—just guide the avatar until it lines up with the edge of the incomplete join."

"Right over here you mean?" Angie worked the joystick back and forth, getting the feel. "This should be easy..."

On the screen, the little avatar moved toward the gap.

"Okay, you're almost there. "You've got to be careful not to touch anything around the gap. That could trigger an alarm."

"Hey!" Angie turned a glare on her companion. "I'm not stupid! I understand what I need to do." She moved the avatar carefully forward, glanced at Sean out of the corner of her eye, and jerked the joystick ever so slightly—just enough to bump the avatar into the edge of the gap.

Everything on the screen froze—and a warning light appeared in the bottom left corner of the screen.

"We've been detected," Sean pushed Angie away and began working on his keyboard. "I've got to disconnect from the internet before they can get a trace."

"Can I do anything?" Angie's face displayed sudden fear. She knew that her father would be enraged if he found out what she was up to.

"Just cross your fingers and hope that I can get us out before they find us." Sean punched two more keys, then the escape key...

The warning light went out.

"I don't think they found us." Sean took a deep breath. "We were lucky."

"Does this mean you can't get to the test?"

"Not tonight," Sean shook his head. "That would be too dangerous." He looked at the girl. "Not tomorrow, either. We have to give them a little time to relax."

"Monday?" Angie frowned. "The test is Wednesday..."

"Monday will work." Sean nodded. "I'll do a little more work over the weekend and make sure we can get through without any problems." He powered his laptop off and loaded it into his bag. "Want to grab a pizza before we go to work?"

"Monday night?" She thought for a moment, then: "Sure—what time?"

"Six—then we can get into the system by seven or so."

"Six o'clock Monday." She leaned down and gave him a quick kiss. "And you're sure it'll work and..." She looked around. "The FBI won't be knocking on my door?"

"It'll work," Sean stood and headed for the door. "And the FBI will stay away."

"Good," Angie gave him a quick hug—enough to make him tingle from head to foot. "Monday night, then."

"Monday." Sean nodded and left, his mind still spinning from that last hug.

***

"Sean?" His mother called as he unlocked the apartment door. "Is that you?"

"It's me, Mom." Sean pulled the door shut and headed for the living room. "I've got a little work to do before..." He stopped short as he saw that his mother was not alone.

"Hi Sean," 'Uncle' Fred Farrell smiled. "You and I need to have a talk." He looked at Lisa and sighed. "Alone would be best."

***

"This one." Ramnarain's finger touched one of the IP addresses on the screen. "I like the interface he used to visualize the firewall."

"But he didn't get in." A slender young man pointed out.

"It was quite obvious that He didn't want to get in." Ramnarain smiled. "I've seen this boy's work before—two or three years ago when I was still working for the government. At the time, he was trying to get into the DOD's personnel files but he wasn't quite able to get through their firewall." He shook his head. "That was the strongest firewall we—and I do mean we—could come up with--and he came within a whisper of getting through. By comparison, the one he was just 'stopped' by might as well have been made of spider webs!" Another

68

shake of the head. "No, he had a reason for stopping." He turned his full attention to the young man. "Find out what it was—we might be able to use the information." He stopped for a moment, thinking. "Take Grant with you. He'll be able to help you bring the boy back here." His forehead wrinkled. "Just don't let him know where he's going—that might create problems we don't want to deal with."

"Okay, Professor." The young man nodded. "I'll take care of it."

***

"And that's the story, Sean." Farrell leaned back in his seat, sipping the coffee that Lisa Piper had provided. "I think that this was done by a small group of young hackers led by Professor Jerry Ramnarain—a computer expert who used to work for us."

"He switched sides?"

"I think he might have," Farrell paused for a long moment. "Although I can't tell you why."

"Okay." Sean thought for a moment. "What do you want me to do?"

"I think he's looking for a new youngster to use in his little hacking team..."

"Why do you think that?"

"Well," Farrell thought for a moment, then: "I...that is, we..."

"You found her!" Sean's tone left no room for disagreement. "What did she have to say?" He looked at Farrell; saw the look that came over his face. "She didn't say anything—she was dead. Killed by this Ramnarain guy."

"Her throat was cut," Farrell looked at the floor. "And her body dumped in the Potomac. We really don't know for sure who was behind it..." He looked up into Sean's eyes. "I won't lie to you—the job might be dangerous. But I think you can handle it." He sighed. "It's the kind of thing your Father wanted you to do."

"Okay," Sean looked at the older man. "I'll do it--but you have to do something for me."

"What?"

"Take care of Mom—get her that pension for her—you know that she deserves it."

"I'll do that whether you agree to work for me or not," Farrell told him. "In fact, I already have my boss looking into it."

"Good," Sean grinned. "So, how do I get this Ramnarain guy to notice me?"

"Just do what you've been doing..." Farrell smiled. "And if you can make it flashier, so much the better..."

***

"Okay, Babe," Sean said to Angie when she answered the door on Monday evening. "I think I've got a way to get what you want." He strolled in past her and pulled his laptop out of its case. "I did some tweaking to my interface and I'm pretty sure that I can get through that firewall this time." He smiled. "And once I've done that, it'll only take a few minutes to copy the Chem test."

"I hope you're right," Angie's face was concerned. "The test is later this week."

"Don't worry," Sean tapped in a series of commands, "Now, this is the firewall..."

The computer screen lit up with a visible, softly glowing, green net.

"This," he plugged in his joystick and moved it just enough to reveal the avatar it controlled—a tiny submarine shape. "Is us."

Angie leaned in close, staring at the screen—and running her breasts across Sean's arm. "We're kind of small..."

"Big things," Sean glanced at Angie's next-to-his-face breasts. "Sometimes come in small passages." He took a deep breath and turned to his joystick. "We just have to find the gap that we noticed the other night..."

"And when we do?"

"We go inside," he glanced at her again. "And get what we want."

Thirty minutes later, they had explored a great deal of net without finding any sort of gap.

"Could they have fixed it?" Angie asked.

"I doubt it. We just have to be patient and..." Sean stopped. "I think..." He maneuvered the little sub to the right. "Yes! There it is!"

"I see it," Angie leaned close, her cheek touching his. "What do we do now?"

"We get in nice and close," he manipulated the joystick carefully, moving the avatar slowly toward the gap. "And then..."

The sub reached the gap in the net, started to pass through...

Just as Angie moved, jostling Sean's arm and sending the tiny submarine right into the side of the gap.

The net turned bright red.

71

"Crap!" Sean pulled the avatar back and unplugged the joystick. "That set off alarms all over the net! We've got to close down and lay low..."

"Whatever you say." Angie moved a bit closer, making it hard for Sean to finish disengaging from the dark net. He had just cut power when there was a knock on the Apartment door.

Sean's head snapped around. "I thought your mother was out for the evening!"

"She is—I don't expect her back until after dinner."

"This is the FBI!" A hard-sounding female voice announced from the hallway. "We know you're in there. Open up before we break the door down!"

"Uh oh." Sean scooped up the laptop and jammed it into his bag. "If they find this in here, we'll both be in trouble!" He pulled the strap over his shoulder. "I'll call you soon!" He stooped and, before she could react, gave her a quick kiss. "'Bye"

Sean smiled and raced away from the apartment door, never looking back. Had he done so, he'd have seen Angie open the door and smile at the good-looking young woman standing there.

"He's heading out the back—just like you figured."

"Good," the young woman nodded. "We have that covered." She held out a sheaf of folded papers. "I believe these are the tests you wanted?"

"Yeah!" Angie leafed through them, checking each one. "Thanks!"

"No problem." The woman gave her a half-wave. "Thanks for co-operating."

Before Angie could speak, the 'agent' had turned away and disappeared down the hallway.

Sean, in the meantime, had ducked out the back window and jumped onto the fire escape, going up toward the roof rather than going down to the street below.

They'll watch the alleyway. He paused to take a quick look down, searching for any unusual movement.

There was none.

Just because I can't see anyone doesn't mean they're not there! He kept climbing. Twelve stories to the roof! Sean shook his head. I hope these are Ramnarain's men and not the real FBI. He grinned. That would be a real kick in the teeth!

It only took a few minutes for Sean to get up the final ladder, over the lip, and onto the roof.

The bridge looks pretty busy. He ran an appraising eye over the bumper-to-bumper traffic on the nearby George Washington Bridge. Must be later then I thought.

Fort Washington Park had started life as a haven for the richest denizens of the city—a way for them to get away from the heat and humidity of downtown Manhattan on the green banks of the Hudson River. They had built some beautiful mansions—mansions which, when air conditioning allowed their owners to move to greener and more remote pastures, were sold and converted to other uses.

They became large multi-room apartments for the middle class at first, then, when those tenants fled to the suburbs, the apartments were cut into smaller, more crowded units for lower income tenants.

At the same time, the spacious yards and tree-filled parks that had originally surrounded these grand but rapidly deteriorating buildings were re-zoned and turned into even more apartment buildings—custom designed to warehouse large numbers of low-income families.

These new buildings were gigantic boxes that shoehorned hundreds of families into the available—and quite often vertical—land space.

The rooftops of these mis-matched buildings stretched out in front of Sean, an unending desert of cement, gravel, and dilapidated shingles.

If I head uptown to 201st, I should be able to climb down behind the subway station and duck underground—blend in with the strap-hangers. Sean began moving. That'll get me out of the area before Angie rats me out. He grinned as he jumped from roof to roof, moving north until he reached the ladder he wanted and began clambering down. The blonde girl was certainly a looker—and Sean could think of many things he'd like to do with her—but trusting her wasn't one of them.

One of these days I'll find a girl with looks and brains! As the thought crossed his mind, Sean's sneakers hit the ground and he turned to head for the subway.

"I assume you're Sean Piper." The youngster skidded to a stop as a burly man dressed in a cheap suit stepped into the alley, blocking his way entrance. "You're bigger than I expected." The man stepped forward and patted Sean's shoulder with a seemingly open hand. "This should make things easier..."

Sean felt the prick of a needle, then nothing at all.

CHAPTER SEVEN

UNKNOWN LOCATION--ONE DAY LATER

"This is the new one we spoke of." Ramnarain gestured toward an unmoving form lying on the white-sheeted bed before them. "I think he'll fit right in—his mother has been cheated by the government and, as you saw, he has found a quite ingenious way to configure his computer with simulation technology."

"He's pretty young." Waterson shook her head, unhappy.

"As I have told you time and again," Ramnarain smiled. "Young is better for our purposes—and this particular young man has a great deal of potential—far too much to allow to go to waste."

"You're right about that." Waterson stood up. "Keep him here for the moment. I'll be back in a few hours and we can discuss recruitment then."

"As you say, Ms. Waterson." The scientist followed her out into the corridor that led to their offices. As he shut the door, he gave his would-be new recruit one last look. "As you say."

***

Those must be the people Uncle Fred wanted to find! Sean had awakened several minutes before the two unknowns had entered his room. He'd seen that he wasn't in a cell—and decided to play possum and see what he could learn. And they want to recruit me—just as he figured!

Sean almost smiled—it was perfect although he hadn't liked the sound of the man's voice--it had been cold and clinical—the voice of someone who just didn't care about anything except his own experiments—a scientist observing a lab rat. I've got to find a way to let Uncle Fred know where I am!

Sean smiled to himself. As soon as I figure that out for myself!

The room, he saw when he finally opened his eyes, was empty aside from the bed he was lying in. There was not another visible piece of furniture—no chair, no bedside table...

No window.

Nice place. Sean sat up and rubbed sleep out of his eyes. I don't think I want to spend too much time here! He threw the covers off and found that he was still completely clothes—save for his shoes.

Under the bed, maybe?

He sat up and hung his legs over the side.

And held onto the sheets for dear life as the room whirled around him.

Whoa! He put his hand over his eyes. Good drugs! I wonder what they used? He closed his eyes tight. And more importantly, how long it's going to take for them to wear off!

He knew he couldn't do anything in this condition so he stayed on the edge of the bed, put his head down, and waited for his mind to clear ...

***

"All right, ladies and gentlemen," Ramnarain strolled into a large room furnished with a dozen or so desks, each with a desktop computer. "I believe it

77

is time to try out our new program." He smiled. "Michael, perhaps you would do the honors?"

"A pleasure, sir." The young man called 'Michael' was of medium height and appeared to be slightly overweight. He had nondescript brown hair and just the hint of a mustache. "Target?"

"As we discussed," Ramnarain smiled. "Transportation is to be our first priority…"

"Yes sir," Michael turned to the intently-watching figures at the other desks. "All right, people, everything is loaded. On my mark…" Michael looked at his own computer, punched in a series of commands. "Mark!"

The room filled with the tiny, insect-like sound of fingers rapidly typing on computer keyboards…

***

WATERSON'S OFFICE--UNKNOWN LOCATION
ONE HOUR LATER

"Did it work?" Alicia Waterson stared at the TV, turned to 'CNN HEADLINE NEWS'. The hosts there had just interviewed a young scientist from NASA about a leaked breakthrough in propulsion and were teasing their next guest—a former 'American Idol' winner who was going to talk about the cancellation of the show. "They should have a report about at least one of the events by now."

"They have nothing to report," Ramnarain examined some code on his laptop. "We failed to connect to the Bluetooth devices" Something caught his eye. "There must be a fault in the coding…"

"So nothing happened!" Ms. Waterson glared at Ramnarain. "You couldn't get through!"

"For the moment." the scientist shrugged. "It won't take long to find the bug and afterwards we can do give them something to worry about..."

Ramnarain stood up and walked to the coffee maker where he poured himself a cup of boiling water and took a tea bag. "Aside from this 'American Idol' nonsense." "

"So what do we do?"

"We try again of course—and again, and again...." Ramnarain added cream and sugar. "There is no other way for us to get our revenge, is there?"

"Our clients don't care about our need for revenge—they just want to get the results we promised." Waterson turned the television off. "They will not be happy with failures of this sort."

"It was only a first attempt," Ramnarain sipped the tea. "There was always the possibility that it wouldn't work the way we planned."

"How long before we're ready to try again?"

"A few days at most." He looked at his companion. "Not more than that." He took a sip. "Our new recruit might be able to help—his use of gaming interfaces is truly out-of-the-box thinking—he might see something we do not."

"You really think that stupid game interface is better than the entry points we're using already?"

"Not better," Ramnarain emptied his cup. "Different." He set the empty crockery down on the counter. "And different, in this line of work, is always better."

"Do you understand how he built the interface?"

"Of course I understand it!" Ramnarain smiled. "But I would prefer to have him present it to us— that would allow him to take credit for the achievement—it is, after all, quite a brilliant concept—and with praise and proper training, he might be capable of much more."

"When do you plan to speak to him?"

"I would like him to meet the others first—get an idea of the layout here." Ramnarain glanced at his watch. "It's almost time for dinner. Suppose we have Mike and Carole Lynne take him to the dining hall and perform the necessary introductions."

"You think that will help?"

"I don't know, but..." Ramnarain gave another of his signature shrugs. "But I am sure that it cannot hurt."

***

PIPER'S ROOM-UNKNOWN LOCATION

Sean Piper was growing very restless. The drug-induced lethargy had worn off hours ago and Sean had been able to explore the room.

There wasn't much to see. A doorway in the far wall opened into a compact bathroom with a sink and toilet. The faucet dispensed very cold water—which pleased Sean as he was incredibly thirsty—perhaps a result of the drug, perhaps simple dehydration. In any case, he was happy to get a drink. There were no glasses—not even paper ones—in the room so he simply turned the cold water on and bent over to slurp it from the tap.

Afterwards, he emptied his bladder and returned to the bed. There was nothing else to do. The room had no television, no computer, no window and, not surprisingly, the only door was locked from the outside.

He lay back, stared at the ceiling and wondered what would happen next.

A moment later, that question was answered by a knock on the door.

"Come on in," Sean shouted out. "It's not as if I can stop you!"

A moment later the door opened and two people entered. A young man--shorter and a bit heavier than Sean, entered first followed by a rather wide young woman.

Mom would call her plump, Sean thought, smiling.

The girl smiled back, pushing back a shock of flaming red hair as she did so. She gave her companion a nudge...

"I'm Michael," the young man so cued blurted out. "Call me Mike—everyone else does."

"Mike," Sean nodded and looked toward the girl.

"This is Carole Lynne," Mike nodded as the young woman stepped forward with hand outstretched.

"Carole." Sean took her hand and shook it as he met her bright brown eyes. "Nice to meet you both." He looked at the pair. "Now, perhaps you'll tell me what I'm doing here?" Sean shook his head. "And maybe you can fill me in on where 'here' is?"

"Yeah, as to that..." Mike bit his lip. "We can't tell you too much just yet. That's up to Dr.

Ramnarain." He looked at Sean. "Although I can promise that He'll tell you everything real soon."

"Ramnarain?"

"He runs the facility." Mike gestured toward the door. "But you'll find out all about that later— we just came to invite you to join us in the common room for dinner."

Sean's stomach suddenly growled—loudly.

"I see that you're hungry!" Mike grinned. "So I guess you'll come?"

"Yeah," Sean shrugged. "I haven't eaten since..." He frowned. "You know, I don't know what time it is or how long it's been since I ate last..."

"Dr. Ramnarain will tell you everything you need to know about stuff like that. For the moment," Mike gestured again. "Come with us?"

Sean nodded assent and followed the two young people through a maze of hallways and corridors until they finally reached a large area they referred to as 'the living area'. They guided him down a corridor that contained a row of small dormitory-style apartments and showed him which ones they lived in before stopping in front of a similar room a few doors away.

"This one is yours," Mike said.

"Temporarily," Carole added. "It'll be permanent when Dr. Ramnarain approves your joining us."

"And before we get some food," Mike told him, swinging the door open. "It might be a good idea for you to take a shower and change."

"Yeah," Carole wrinkled her nose. "You're kind of ripe."

"We'll meet you back here in fifteen minutes." Mike told him.

"Don't dawdle!" Carole added.

Sean took the hint and, after shutting the door behind them, headed for the shower.

It had, he learned, very good flow and very hot water that came from a shower head set at a good height for someone of Sean's size. He had grown used to bending over to wash his hair, here, he could stand up straight and have a little room to spare.

After toweling off, Sean checked the clothing in the closet and chest of drawers. He wasn't surprised to find that the clothing sizes were all correct. I'm a little taller than most kids my age, he thought, looking at the shirt. But they allowed for that... He ran a hand through his hair. I guess they measured me while I was unconscious.

The room itself was quite comfortable. Aside from the nicely equipped bathroom and 'en suite' bedroom, there was a small living area that featured a comfortable couch placed in front of a large flat-screen TV equipped with a DVD player.

There was a compact home office set-up across the room, complete with a top-of-the-line desktop computer.

But no internet connection, Sean discovered upon booting up the machine.

Sean looked the whole place over and realized, with some surprise, that it was larger than the New York City apartment he had been sharing with his mom and sister!

There's real money at work here, he thought as he looked around the living area. I wonder what the plan to buy with their investment?

He still had a couple of minutes before Mike and Carole were due so Sean made a quick scan of the entire apartment, searching for hidden cameras or other surveillance gear.

He didn't find anything that looked unusual or suspicious—which told him absolutely nothing.

Spy-cams have gotten so small, he knew. That I might not spot one even if it was right in front of me! And after all, he smiled and shrugged. It's not like I could do anything about it if I found one!

When the expected knock on the door came, Sean joined Carole and Mike for a short walk that led to a branching corridor.

Sean counted the doors on each side of the hall as he went.

Twenty doors, he wondered if that meant there were twenty kids living here. I'll have to find out!

They crossed a bisecting hallway and Mike nodded to one side. "The computer room is down there—you're not allowed there yet."

"I know," Sean nodded. "Not until Dr. Ramnarain approves me."

"You got it!" Mike grinned.

"So where can I go?"

"Anywhere else in the compound." Carole gestured. "Including the theater, common rooms, and cafeteria." She pointed in front of them. "Which are all right at the end of this corridor."

A moment later, she smiled and nodded as the corridor opened up into quite a large space--the 'Common Room'.

A couch, television, and small 'coffee' tables with various game consoles and magazines were set on one side of the room, creating an open square. On the opposite side was a long counter where, Mike told him, food was available at set times-- cafeteria style.

Filling the area between the counter and the square of gaming equipment was a dining area filled with tables and chairs.

Sean nodded and took a long look at the large and well-equipped kitchen that stood behind the serving counter.

I wonder who does the cooking, he asked himself. I hope they don't expect me to help—I burn water!

There was quite a variety of foods on the serving bar---more than enough choices for Sean. I hope everything tastes as good as it looks, he thought as he piled mashed potatoes next to the large chunk of prime rib that half-filled his plate. He surveyed the large eating area which had clearly been built for far more people than were now using it. This is big enough for fifty or so, Sean estimated. Now, he counted heads, there are only about ten people.

He knew, of course, that there could easily be many more people living here—he had no idea just how big the complex was. There could well be several other dormitory areas down corridors he hadn't yet explored.

But that was for later—now it was time to eat! He had known he was hungry but now, with the smell of food all around him he realized just how hungry he really was!

When did I have my last meal? He wondered. He could remember a hot dog he'd scarfed down on his way to Angie's...

There's no way to know how long ago that was—I don't know how long it took to bring me here or how long I was asleep. He grabbed a roll off the counter and quickly gobbled it down. I can't worry about that now. It's more important to find out what these people want. He smiled ruefully. After I get some food inside me!

Mike and Carole showed him to a table on the far right-hand side of the room. Four other young people were seated there, each within a year or two of Sean's age. Carole waved for Mike to do the introductions.

"Hey, everyone." The young man laid a hand on Sean's shoulder. "This is Sean—you've all heard about him."

Three of the faces swiveled in his direction and Sean thought it polite to give them a nod in return. He waited while Mike to the other side of the table and stood behind each of the young people in turn. "This is Jayson". He indicated a slender black young man of medium height who, to Sean's eyes, seemed to be several years older than the others. He's at least twenty two or three, Sean thought. The others are around my age. He looked Jayson over. I wonder why there's such an age difference.

Jayson glanced indifferently at Sean, nodded once, and then went back to the book he was reading.

"Bob." Sean moved along to an eighteen-year old of average height and slightly above average weight who smiled and waved with one hand while continuing to eat with the other.

"Dona" A rather drab girl of nineteen or so kept her eyes down on her food and quietly waved at Sean, never once meeting his eyes or, for that matter, looking up.

"Last but not least, Halle."

Sean's heart skipped a beat as the indicated girl met his eyes. *God, she's gorgeous!* Halle looked to be about nineteen years old and roughly the same size and shape as Angie—but where Angie had been blond and pretty in a blue-eyed, girl-next-door sort of way, Halle was dark and dangerous beautiful with flashing black eyes and skin the color of coffee. *I'd sure like to get to know her better!* Sean dropped into the seat next to her, ignoring Mike's obvious attempt to get him to join he and Carole.

"So." He was glad his voice hadn't decided to break just then. "What are you...?" He quickly looked up and down the table. "What are all of you in for?"

"In for?" Jayson was a few inches shorter then Sean but had the aspect of one looking down his nose at him as he answered. "We're not imprisoned--this isn't a jail!"

"Well," Mike, now seated across from Sean, put his fork down and smiled sheepishly. "Not exactly."

"Come on." Sean looked down the row of faces. "Nobody just recruits kids our age unless there's a good reason to do so."

"Such as?" Jayson was even more obviously looking down his nose now.

"I don't know." Sean met the other boy's glare with one of his own. "If I had to guess, I'd say embezzlement, hacking, theft of services—computer crimes."

"Good guess." Mike nodded as he ate. "I did manage to get a little extra money out of my neighborhood ATM." He smiled at Sean. "About $50,000 worth." He nodded toward Carole. "My girlfriend here got a bit more."

"About triple." Carole shook her head as she said the word. "Then, when she found out, my mother turned me in and gave it all back!"

"Dona was able to access the Pentagon mainframe." Sean raised an eyebrow—he had tried that firewall himself and it had been hefty enough to get him to back away! "And promptly issued discharge orders to every single member of the Army, Navy, and Air Force."

"I hate wars and killing." Dona spoke with eyes still downcast. "I figured it would be tough for this country to go to war if they had no soldiers." Her mouth hardened. "But nobody paid any attention to the orders—they just showed them to their bosses and laughed! She shook her head. "Fools!"

"Okay..." Mike shrugged. "Bob here has never told us how or why he was recruited.

"That's because it's none of your damn business!" The boy continued to chew away at his dinner as if he had not been interrupted.

"Finally, Jayson and Halle." Mike gestured to the two seated to Sean's left. "Who, as Jayson was so quick to tell you a moment ago, have done nothing at all."

He smiled at Sean's blank look.

"They're volunteers!" Mike shook his head in amazement at the thought. "They were both students of the good Doctor and volunteered to come here with him!"

"Why wouldn't I choose to work with Dr. Ramnarain?" Halle's voice was smooth and light—with a sort of husky lilt that made Sean's skin tingle. "After all, he's the number one man in his field—and this work is far more interesting than anything I could have found at the college," she flashed a conspiratorial smile at Sean. "Not to mention being far more rewarding—in all kinds of ways!"

Sean's blank look became more pronounced.

The girl turned toward Mike. "Doesn't he know what we do?"

Mike shook his head. "Not yet." He looked at all of them. "And the Doc doesn't want him to have any details until he decides whether we're going to recruit him or not."

"I can see why they haven't yet made a decision on this one." Jayson gave Sean another of his downward glances. "He is, after all, a mere child." He looked at his watch and stood up. "One with whom we've already wasted far too much time." He ran his eyes over the others. "The film I downloaded is ready to go in the theater—shall we go and watch it?"

Sean carefully kept his expression neutral as the others stood. Bob gave a curt nod and grabbed one last roll before turning to follow Jayson. Dona kept her head down and her hands at her side as she wandered off.

Come on, Halle! Sean turned to the girl as Jayson called her. Give me something—some sign that you know I exist! He smiled as a line came into his head. Give me some sugar! Sean loved the Evil Dead films and Bruce Campbell was one of his idols. At least say something to me!

The dark girl stood and took her place next to Jayson who put a possessive hand over her shoulder, all but sneering at Sean as he did so. As one, they turned to leave...

Halle stopped, and turned toward Sean. She looked him right in the eye and spoke: "See you later, Sean."

She smiled at him before turning to join Jayson.

***

The remainder of the meal was anticlimactic. Mike and Carole stayed with Sean, making small talk that carefully avoided any indications of the purpose of the complex or what the other young people did.

Sean listened and watched as a few other people moved up and down the long corridor.

A few stayed to eat—but none of them were anywhere near the age of the kids and each came and went as quickly as possible.

They're all over thirty, Sean told himself. And clearly not here to do the same work as Halle and the others. He glanced over at Mike and Carole. These two know what's going on. He frowned. But they're afraid to tell me without permission. He took a moment to return to the serving counter where he cut off a large slice of apple pie, and dumped a scoop of vanilla ice-cream on top. I guess I'm going to have to find out on my own.

After dinner, Mike showed Sean the 'day room'--the partitioned-off area that sat opposite the cafeteria. Sean had already noted its big-screen, state of the art flat-screen TV and now he was shown a brand-new Blu-Ray player; a top of the line surround-sound system; and a gaming system complete with a suite of cutting-edge games. Mike invited him to play a round of 'Call of Duty', but, after a few minutes of play, Sean threw up his hands. "Sorry, man. I guess it's all catching up to me now that my belly's full!" He yawned.

"It's my fault." Mike looked embarrassed. "I should have thought about that." He saved the game with a quick motion and stood. "C'mon," he headed for the door. "I'll take you back to your room—I doubt you'd be able to remember the way yet."

The other young man was wrong—Sean remembered every step of the way and could have easily found his way back. But I'll keep that to myself, he thought. It might come in handy!

He went over his own memorized route as he followed Mike down the corridor, checking that he really knew the way. Two more rights, he told himself. Then straight down the hall to 'my' room.

Sean smiled as Mike took that exact path.

"Your place is just up here." Mike stopped in front of the door. "Get some rest—we'll all talk in the morning." Mike frowned. "Do you think you can find your way there, or should I meet you here."

"I'll get there." Sean yawned as conspicuously as he dared, and quickly added. "I think."

"Okay." Mike turned back toward his own room. "I'll meet you there." He glanced at a watch. "Say about 9AM?"

"What time is it now?" Sean's own watch showed 11PM. But with a big gap in his memory, he didn't know if he was even in the same time zone.

"It's just turned eleven." Mike looked up. "See you in the morning?"

Sean nodded. "Nine sharp." He opened the door. "Good night."

CHAPTER EIGHT

PIPER'S ROOM-UNKNOWN LOCATION

Sean, essaying another yawn, turned out all the lights in the living area of the little apartment and made his way to the bedroom—just as he would if he were actually planning to go to sleep.

Once at the bed, he sat down, took off his shoes and socks, and, after shutting off the lights, climbed--a bit noisily—under the covers.

Darkness, he hoped, would make the surveillance cameras—if they're actually here—a bit less effective. Pretty soft, he noted as he lay back on the bed, but I can't afford to fall asleep now! He kept his eyes open. I might not wake up in time to do what I have to do!

He waited, going through plans of action one after the other...

When the glowing hands of his watch finally touched at midnight, Sean got up as quietly as he could and padded barefoot to the door, shoes and socks held in his hands to avoid any excess noise.

He slipped silently through the unlocked door into a corridor that was dimly lit and quite deserted.

Everyone must be asleep, he told himself, as he took a second to pull his shoes. Ready, he walked—as quietly as he could— down the long corridor that, he knew, led away from the common room and toward the computer lab where, he hoped and believed he'd find the answers he'd come for.

Right turn here, he remembered, then ahead about fifty paces…

Moments later, Sean found himself standing in front of an unmarked door that he knew had to be the computer lab. It had no knob, just a keypad set in the wall to the right.

Crap, he thought. I have no way to figure out the combination! He knew that most places used something simple, something everyone could remember…

But I have no idea of what the people here have in common. Sean stared at the keypad. There's no way to work anything out. I'll have to wait until…

There was a hiss as an unseen mechanism went into action—loud enough to get Sean to take a long step back into the shadows where he watched the door slide open.

Nobody came out.

It seems like somebody's giving me an invitation to enter, Sean thought, then grinned. It'd be rude not to accept.

He stepped through the door and looked around the room beyond, instantly fascinated.

There were computers everywhere—all makes and models, each of them networked into a group of servers that stood upright in the center of the room.

Lots of processing power. Sean calculated as he bent to examine the closest machine. Let's see what this one can do… He tapped a few keys and smiled when a password screen came up. Trusting souls…

"The others value their privacy," a familiar voice came from behind. "And I do my best not to pry."

Sean froze, surprised. *I didn't hear the door open!*

"You're wondering why you didn't hear the door." Footsteps sounded on the tile floor behind him. "It's because I didn't come that way." The steps came closer. "I was already inside—catching up on some work in the observation station that lies just beyond the wall over there." The voice was getting closer. "I was, in point of fact, killing time while I waited for you to arrive."

Sean whirled around and found himself facing a slender man wearing a light blue shirt under a spotlessly-white lab coat.

"I knew you wouldn't have any trouble finding your way here." The man smiled a smile so knowing and confident that Sean found it just a tiny bit unsettling. "After all, spatial coordination is a common gift for people like us." The smile grew, showing perfect white teeth. "I am, if you haven't already guessed, Dr. Ramnarain and I believe I am in a position to offer you a rather interesting," the smile widened. "And extremely lucrative position with my little organization."

CHAPTER NINE

FORT WASHINGTON PARK, NEW YORK

"Frank!" Lisa Piper threw herself into Farrell's arms. "Thank God you came!"

"It's all right," He patted the slender woman on the back. "Everything is all right..."

"No!" she pushed herself away and looked at him with eyes full of appeal. "Sean didn't come home last night—or the night before." She looked at him. "Do you know where he is?"

"Not exactly." Farrell bit his lower lip. "Although I'm sure he's all right..."

"You sent him out on that job, didn't you!"

"I..." Farrell hesitated. "You didn't go to the police, did you?"

"Of course I did," she shook her head. "But they won't even let me fill out a report until at least forty-eight hours have passed and they didn't really act as if they were going to try very hard to find him."

"It's probably a good thing that you go in tomorrow and fill out a report—we should at least appear to be looking for him."

"I am looking for him!" She glared at Farrell. "And unless you tell me that you know where he is, I'm going to continue to look!"

Farrell nodded. "Good, that's good. If they check..."

"If who checks!" Lisa's eyes locked on Frank's. "Franklyn Fitzgerald Farrell, just what are you up to—and what have you done with my son!"

"I gave Sean a job." Frank looked around the tiny apartment. "He wanted to help and I needed someone like him."

"And you didn't ask me?"

"He's eighteen now—a full-grown man..."

"He's my son! Hell, he's Robert's son!" She began to cry. "You should have told me what you wanted him for!" She rubbed her eyes.

"Sean will be fine, Lisa. He's a smart young man—and very capable..."

"Capable of what!" The tears stopped, replaced by a glare that would have driven a lesser man away."

"We have a problem with some computer hackers. Sean's good with computers..."

"Is that why you sent him that laptop?" The glare grew deadlier. "So he'd be ready for this kind of mission?"

"Well..."

"Get out of here." Lisa shook her head. "Get out now!"

"But..."

"Get out and don't come back without Sean." Her gaze burned into him. "You hear me? Come back with Sean or don't come back at all!"

Farrell nodded once and left, closing the door quietly behind him.

CHAPTER TEN

RAMNARAIN'S OFFICE-UNKNOWN
LOCATION

"Let me see if I understand what you're asking me to do," Sean said, eyes on the older man form before him. "You want me to help you and the others find ways through firewalls and other computer protective systems." Sean saw the Doctor smile and nod. "Why?"

"Two reasons," Ramnarain turned and gestured for Sean to follow him into the observation room. Once inside, he pointed his visitor to a comfortably upholstered seat before settling into a similar seat behind the large desk that covered the area in front of the far wall. "First, you should be aware that large corporations and institutions of all kinds routinely pay groups like ours to find weaknesses in their cyber-protection."

"Yeah," Sean nodded. "I think I read that somewhere..."

"It's far less expensive than letting the so-called 'black hat hackers' get into their databases." Ramnarain smiled. "You'd be surprised to know just how much money we're talking about."

"You said there was a second reason..."

"We'll discuss that later," Ramnarain settled back into his seat. "First, I want to discuss your little submarine simulation..."

"That?" Sean shook his head. "It's nothing! I just set up an interface that translates base data into imagery—you use the navigation program to pick an HTML and it puts you just outside the web address in question, if there's a firewall of any kind, it appears as a net or a gate or a fence..."

"And once you can see that, you can explore the image until you find a weakness and slip through," Ramnarain nodded. "I've had a look at the interface program. It's brilliantly conceived— the concept of using a gaming program to visualize firewalls and anti-worm programs..." He shook his head. "I never would have attempted to solve those problems that way!"

Sean shrugged. "Humans think in visual terms—it seemed obvious to me that problems like hacking through a firewall could be simplified if you could see the wall rather than line after line of computer code."

"It's brilliant!" Ramnarain leaned forward. "I would love to have a brain like yours working with me. It's rare for someone so intelligent to be capable of thinking so far out of the box.

Join us." He looked into Sean's eyes. "What would you say to a base annual salary of one-hundred twenty-five thousand dollars?"

"A hundred and twenty-five..."

"There are bonuses as well—and various other incentives."

An image of Halle appeared in Sean's head. Is she one of the incentives? He wondered.

"Join us, Sean. Think of what that money would mean to your mother..." Ramnarain leaned closer. "And your sister." He nodded. "I know she needs an operation and it's going to be expensive— far too expensive for your mother to afford..."

Sean bit into his lower lip. That's true enough, he thought. Kathleen would soon need another operation.

And it would be nice to get her and Mom a nicer place to live…

"I'm interested," Sean said. "But I have one question."

"Yes?"

"You said there were two sources of income," Sean looked into the Doctor's eyes. "What's the second one?"

"Asking that question means you've already guessed the answer," Ramnarain's smile broadened. "We create—under contract you might say—very specialized worms."

"Worms to attack what?"

Ramnarain shrugged. "That depends. Air Traffic Control, Electrical grids, water treatment facilities." He looked at Sean. "Whatever the client wants."

"And you're not too picky about the client, are you?"

"Not picky at all." Ramnarain's smile remained intact. "If you want, I'll let Halle fill you in on some of the evils perpetrated by the companies and countries we attack. Perhaps she can convince you that it's the right thing to do."

"Perhaps…" Sean held his face as blank as he could, his mind racing. "I'm going to need a little time to think all this over…"

"Of course!" Ramnarain stood and waited for Sean to do likewise. "Take all the time you need—just remember, your sister isn't getting any better," he looked into Sean's eyes. "And by this time, your mother must be very concerned about you!"

Sean kept his poker face in place and walked to the door, his mind racing through his various plans of action. What's the best thing for me to do? He nodded and waved as Doctor Ramnarain opened the door for him. Do I take the job—join these people. The money would mean a lot to Mom and Kathleen...

Or do I finish the job Frank sent me to do. Find out where I am and pass that location to him?

He immediately knew the answer—and realized that he had known it all along.

It's payment for hurting people. He shook his head. Blood money.

He suspected that attacks on the United States would be high on the to-do lists of the kind of clients Ramnarain must have.

No, he opened the door to his room and stepped inside. I can't join them. He bit his lip, thinking. So how do I get out and warn Farrell?

He sat down and stared into the darkness, thinking about the problem until, just before dawn, he came to a decision...

CHAPTER ELEVEN

UTILITY CORRIDOR--UNKNOWN
LOCATION

All right, if I have this properly worked out; the next turn should take me to the generator room... Sean quietly made his way down a long corridor, checking what landmarks he had been allowed to see.

After what seemed a very long distance, the corridor intersected with two others. This seems like the right direction. Sean turned right and kept going. This place can't be that big! I should get there in a few minutes...

Sean had spent most of the day after his meeting with Ramnarain hanging around the Common Room, playing games with whoever was free, snacking, and generally lazing around in the way he thought Ramnarain would expect of someone thinking about the good Doctor's offer.

But, if that was truly what Ramnarain expected, he had severely underestimated Sean Piper.

Despite appearances to the contrary, Sean wasn't just idly killing time—he was, in fact, using his position in the center of the facility to observe the movements of the people around him, all the while listening in on their conversations for what bits of information he could glean.

As time passed, he got more and more date— enough to piece together an image of the complex into which he had been taken

Now, after digesting that information, he had made his way deep into the bowels of the place, following the maze of utility corridors that crisscrossed under the main floors. He had eventually reached this corridor--far less finished then the ones above—and the wiring conduits he needed...

There! A series of cables emerged from the finished ceiling and ran toward what had to be the generator room.

If this thing was built when I believe it was, one of those lines will carry the feed from their security cameras. Sean stopped, took a moment to inspect the cables, then, having come to a decision, dug into the pillowcase he had taken from his room and began to pull out the gear he'd need.

Let's see if I've picked the right line! He pulled a bit of broken mirror from the bag and used the jagged edge to scrape the insulation off one of the wires. If he was correct about the color coding being used, this was the lead to the camera system.

He took a wire he had prepared out of his bag. It had an alligator clip at one end and a USB connector at the other. He used the clip to connect to the stripped section of wire before plugging the USB into one of the ports on what had started life as his room's desktop computer.

It was kind of stupid of them to give me so many tools! Sean had removed the computer's guts, discarding the casing and unimportant peripherals to save space and weight. He still had the mother board, power supply, and monitor screen as well as a wireless mouse and various pieces of cable and wire he'd salvaged from what was left. I guess they didn't think that someone would use them this way! There was actually an electrical socket nearby—he really didn't need it, the computer battery was at 100 percent but...

Waste not, want not. Sean plugged in and powered up. He couldn't help but smile as the ragged looking collection of electronic gear-- ugly and misshapen as it was--immediately began its start-up routine. This shouldn't take too long...

It didn't. Less than thirty seconds later, the monitor screen came to life and Sean tapped in a series of commands, allowing him access to the complex's main computer. Once inside, he turned his attention to the internal security system.

Nobody every plans for a hacker who is already inside the network! He thought, smiling.

He was right about that. No alarm sounded as Sean began looking for the security cameras.

There's the feed! He tapped it and looked at an image of a blank corridor. Using that as a base, he began searching all the corridor cameras—and found one that showed the corridor he was using. A few strokes on the keyboard insured that the camera in question would show nothing other than the image of an empty corridor would get to the security office.

Safe for the moment, Sean split his monitor into four quarters and began to explore each of what he now saw were the many security cameras scattered throughout the complex.

Seems like a good idea to check out my back trail before I go any further, he decided. In every game he had ever played, every movie he had ever seen, that was the one thing that was of paramount importance. I'll start with my room, then...

He saw movement on one of the corridor cameras in the dormitory area—he noted that it was the camera closest to his room—and stopped the rotation. That's interesting. He blew the image up to full-screen. I guess the good Doctor doesn't really trust me as much as he indicated. Sean watched as a guard—the same man who'd drugged him in Manhattan—checked his door, making sure it was locked. Eventually they'll take a look inside and find out I'm not there. Sean nodded and checked the next camera in the sequence. Let's not make it easy. He was unsurprised to find a camera in his 'private' space. From the angle, it must be in the light fixture over the bed... He scanned saved video and found footage of him asleep. He instructed the system to play it in a loop. Now it'll just show me sleeping safe and sound in my little room.

Sean smiled and returned to the keyboard, continuing his search through the surveillance systems, accessing camera after camera. He paused for a moment as he reached the one that he knew would be inside Halle's room—and jumped past it. It'd be wrong to sneak a look, he told himself.

It took a few minutes but he kept working his way down empty corridors until he reached his present position, then: Time to check what's up ahead.

There wasn't much beyond the camera he'd already dealt with. Just a couple of motion detectors and a pressure monitor which he quickly took care of.

Okay, he told himself. The motion detectors are on standby. The pressure monitors are set to 'test', he looked over his preparations. That should just about do it! Only one thing left to do...

He typed a long series of commands into the keyboard, nodded when the interface he wanted appeared on the screen and typed in a short phrase. That's all I can do from here—I hope he gets it in time.

Sean took a deep breath, than reached up to unclip his access into the system. A moment later he had unplugged form the socket and loaded all his bits and pieces back into the pillowcase.

I might need them later! He told himself as he tied the case shut and slung it over a shoulder. Then he stepped out and began moving quickly down the now unguarded corridor.

CHAPTER TWELVE

EDGEWATER HOLIDAY INN, EDGEWATER NJ

Farrell was jolted out of sleep by a loud buzz.

A message? He picked up his phone and unlocked it. Who would send me a message at...? He glanced at his watch. Two in the morning!

He looked at the phone—then sat up straight and looked at it again.

Sean's on the loose! He read the message. He wants me to meet him at his Dad's place. Farrell frowned. The apartment? He shook his head. No, he can't mean that, Robert never lived in that apartment... Farrell stared out into the night. So where is his Dad's place?

The answer struck him at that exact moment.

Of course! Farrell climbed out of bed and grabbed his clothes. I'm only about three hours away, if I rush, I can get there before the sun comes up. He clipped his holster to his belt. I hope that's fast enough...

He ran out of the door and headed for his car.

CHAPTER THIRTEEN

WATERSON'S OFFICE-UNKNOWN LOCATION

"One of the guards reported the access to the basement corridors was ajar," Ms. Waterson snarled the words at Ramnarain who sat across from her. She was grumpy—she didn't like it when her sleep was interrupted. "My people are all accounted for—what about your 'students'?"

"You woke me up in the middle of the night for that!" Ramnarain glared at her. "You know that an alarm would have sounded if any of my group tried to leave the compound."

"You're sure of that?"

"Of course I'm sure! I designed the protocols myself! They're foolproof!"

"Nothing is foolproof! That system is run by the computer—and every one of those youngsters is capable of hacking into it and changing your protocols—you've convinced me of that much!" She leaned forward. "I'll ask you again, is everyone still inside the compound?"

Ramnarain's eyes widened as he considered the possibility. He didn't think that any of his young hackers would ever want to leave without permission. But it is possible—and there's the new boy....

He spent several seconds thinking through the possibilities—then nodded and moved to the computer console on her desk. "There's a way to know for certain if everyone is still here." He pulled the keyboard toward him and tapped in a series of instructions. "I installed a computer paradigm that keeps count of the number of people in the complex according to the security system. As a check, I can compare that data with atmosphere usage and ambient body heat—our air-conditioning system monitors both. Any difference will show..." He stared at the screen, stunned by the result.

"You're one short, aren't you?" Waterson squeezed the bridge of her nose between her forefinger and thumb in an attempt to dispel the stress that she could fell building. "I wager it turns out to be young Mr. Piper. I never liked him." She shook her head. "And if he's as smart as you think he is, it's going to be hard to find him before he finds a way to get out of the complex."

Ramnarain's face went pale. "We'll have to put our evacuation plan into effect. Make sure he can't lead anyone back here."

"I'd rather he didn't have the chance to do that."

"What do you mean?" The scientist stared at his superior. "He's gone! All he has to do is reach a store or house that will let him use a telephone..."

"Unless we find him first." Waterson glared at her associate. "By all means prepare to evacuate. If we fail to locate him, we will have no choice but to move everyone and everything to our back-up location." Waterson had forced her face back to calm. "It won't hurt if you begin the process of scrubbing any computers we cannot move. I'll get more of our people looking for him." She picked up her telephone and punched in a series of numbers.

"It's a good thing that he has no way to reach a vehicle. That alone will cut down the distance he can cover."

"It's possible that I have a way to track him," Ramnarain returned to the computer and began entering commands, carefully checking the results. "When he first arrived, we attached a..." He smiled. "Well, you would call it a bug but it is, in reality, nothing more than a simple GPS transmitter." He looked up and smiled. "We embedded it in the tread of his shoes where it's unlikely to be found."

"He's a clever boy—he found a way to get past your security system..." Waterson shook her head. "I can't believe he wouldn't look for something as simple as that!"

"He may not have realized that we would do such a thing—at his age, he can't have much experience in this sort of work..." Ramnarain leaned forward, smiling at his display. "There!" He pointed to a marker on a map. "There he is!" He turned to Waterson. "Before you send in your muscle, give me an opportunity to try something."

"It'd better be good!"

"Oh," Ramnarain smiled. "It will be—I promise that!"

***

OUTSIDE UNKNOWN LOCATION

I don't think I ever saw that many stairs before! It hadn't taken Sean long to find his way to the emergency exit in the generator room. A door there (opened with the aid of his computer) took him to a staircase that, he knew from the warning signs, would lead him to the surface.

It had, however, been a very long climb.

Well, there was that visit to the Empire State Building. He grinned. But I took the elevator up!

He looked around, scanning the darkness around him. The staircase had ended in a concealed doorway opening onto a large open field. Foliage grew everywhere and a copse of large trees was just a few yards from the exit.

There wasn't a house or road in sight.

He looked up at the panorama of stars overhead and remembered the stellar navigation course he'd taken the year his dad had been stationed in North Carolina. Mom thought it was a waste of time, but...

He studied the constellations as he recalled what he'd learned ...

I'm still in the US. Sean stared at the sky. On the East Coast—Virginia, maybe. Or Maryland. He nodded. Pretty much where I expected...

He hadn't been able to access the internet through his computer while inside the complex— and he didn't want to take the time to assemble it and try now.

I can use the stars, he nodded. I don't need the internet. He studied the sky. North is over that way. Sean's eyes traced a line from the big dipper to the North Star. I want to go east, he aligned himself carefully. They'll be checking out this exit before too long. He started to walk. I'd better be pretty far away when they do. He glanced up, picked a star that was oriented in the right direction. If I keep going this way, sooner or later, I'll hit water. He grinned wryly as he passed the tree line and darkness closed in around him. I just hope it's the water I expect it to be!

Sean walked in silence, thinking of what Ramnarain had offered him. Maybe I should have taken the money, he thought. Kathleen needs the operation and Mom... His throat tightened as he thought about how worried his mother must be. I'll find a road soon, he told himself. And that will lead me to a telephone. He sped up just a little. It's only a matter of time...

Shortly thereafter, Sean did find roads—a number of them—but they were minor county roads—one or two lanes wide and unlikely to take him where he wanted to go. Their markers, however, told him that he was right about one thing—he was in Northern Virginia...

Three hours later, he came across something that proved he was right about something else...

That's a city! He stopped and studied the faint glow of lights on the horizon. A big city! I'll be able to reach home from there. Tell Mom where I am! Not to mention...

He'd been counting his paces as best he could and thought he'd come around 14 miles so far.

I should be able to lead the authorities back to Ramnarain's lair easily enough. Sean thought—and had a sudden pang of guilt—which he quickly dispelled. I don't know what they have in mind... He thought as he carefully crossed a single lane road. But I know they've got to be stopped!

He spied a long wall ahead of him, one that disappeared into the trees in either direction. He'd seen quite a few fences along his route—some of them little more than rusty barbed wire strung between rotting wooden posts.

This one was different.

It's old! Brick and mortar! Sean looked it over. And it goes on for quite a ways in either direction. He grinned. Was my navigation that good? He touched the gritty stone of the wall. Maybe I learned more in that class than I thought...

He stepped back into the middle of the road and spent a long moment scanning the entire area around him, slowly turning in a circle. He was trying to see if anything was moving...

There was nothing.

I guess I'm really in the clear! Sean returned to the base of the wall and ran his fingertips across it. This might not be the right place—but right or wrong, I'm going to have to climb over to know for sure. He felt old mortar crumble at his touch. This is certainly old enough and.... He glanced to the top. If it's what I think it is, it won't have pressure sensors on the top. He grinned. Or ribbon wire! He shrugged. I don't have the time to work my way all the way around to the front gates—always assuming this is the right place and there are gates. He looked behind him. I'm going to have to chance climbing over...

He let the pillowcase slide off his back and, not giving himself time to overthink things, tossed it over the fence, suppressing a wince as he heard it crash down on the other side.

I Hope nothing got too smashed up! He took one last look around—then backed off a few paces and ran straight at the wall, jumping as high as he could—and was surprised when his hands closed over the very top. Didn't think I could do that, he grinned. Must be more scared than I thought...

For a long second, loose mortar and dirt slipping under his fingers made him think he might fall off but, finally, he managed to get a toe into a gap. That gave him the purchase he needed to pull himself up onto the top. He squatted there for a long moment, studying the landscape spread out before him.

Then he dropped down onto the rolling green grass below, landing barely a foot from his pillowcase.

All right, Sean took the time to open the bag and quickly inspect what was inside. Nothing looks too badly damaged. He re-tied the mouth of the pillowcase and hoisted it back over his shoulder before trotting between the rows of gravestones that ran across the landscape in front of him. Now, let's see if I really did get the navigation right!

Sean entered the forest of granite and marble, following a track marked by signs and arrows until he found the section he wanted.

Then he stepped onto the grass, looking for one specific marker...

And froze in his tracks.

"Hey there, Sean." Halle stood ten yards in front of him, a nasty smile on her face. "Happy to see me?"

CHAPTER FOURTEEN

INTERSTATE 95--TEN MILES FROM BALTIMORE MD.

I'm not going to make it, Farrell thought as he sped down I-95 toward the Washington beltway. I'm going to be late!

He'd been stopped by a Highway Patrolman while cruising down the Jersey Turnpike—the officer in question had refused to release him even when Farrell showed him his DHS credentials.

Farrell had considered just brushing the officer aside and driving away—but soon realized that, while that would work just fine in some parts of the world, here in the US homeland, it would only lead to bigger problems.

So he waited, fuming, while the officer wrote a speeding ticket (very markedly taking his time). When it was finished, Farrell took it, wrote the young man's badge number on the face of it, and shoved the flimsy paper into his glove box.

Guy's got balls, Farrell thought as he drove away. Might be worth a closer look—when I have the time!

Right now, Farrell had to get to Washington—and fast! He put his foot down hard and did his best to make up lost time...

***

ARLINGTON NATIONAL CEMETARY-ARLINGTON VA.

"This is why I left," Sean led Halle along a grassy trail and into an area full of small white tombstones. "I wanted to talk to my Father before I made a decision."

"Your father?"

"Right there," Sean nodded toward one of the stones.

"Oh," Halle saw the name: Robert A. Piper chiseled into the marble. "I see..."

"It's been a while since I came here," he shrugged. "It's a bit of a journey."

"How did you know the compound was anywhere near Arlington?"

"I went into the kitchen and took a look around." He smiled. "Most of the food there was brand-name—but some of the fresh stuff—like the milk and vegetables—was regional with packaging showing it came from Northern Virginia."

"I never thought of that..."

"I knew that once I got out of the compound, all I had to do was travel East—eventually, I'd have to hit the Potomac River and from there..." He shrugged again. "I could find my way here." He looked down at the marker. "I was surprised how easily I found the fence—I knew it was the one around Arlington National Cemetery as soon as I saw it. Now," he looked at her. "Tell me how you found me?"

"There's a tracker chip in your sneaker," she smiled. "Easy to follow."

"I should have thought of checking for something like that." He looked at her. "What now?"

"We've decided you can't be trusted, so…"

Jayson stepped out from behind a tree, a shiny-bladed Buck knife in his hand.

"It's time for you to join your father."

***

The rear end of Farrell's car skidded across loose gravel as he braked into an open spot just outside the main entrance to Arlington National. The gates wouldn't open for another two and a half hours—but Farrell didn't plan to wait.

I have a bad feeling about this whole situation, he thought as he made an automatic check of the magazine in his Glock. Sean's disappearance smells—he'd have contacted me if he'd made direct contact with Ramnarain which means that he was grabbed—-and I'd bet that girl of his had something to do with it. He holstered the pistol and locked the car before heading for the Cemetery entrance. But that's for later—for right now, the big question is—am I in the right place?

He climbed over the main gate and headed for the area where Robert Piper had been interned.

I just hope Sean is there to tell me I figured it out!

***

Sean wasn't too shocked to see Jayson—the slender young man was never far from Halle's side.

He was, however, a bit surprised to see the knife.

"Just what do you two have in mind?" Sean was careful to keep his voice level—unafraid and unworried. Never let them see you sweat, he thought. Dad used to say that.

117

"I'm going to cut out your traitorous guts," Jayson glanced at Halle who nodded. "You little piece of crap!"

Sean allowed a faint smile to cross his lips. He'd been practicing various fighting skills since he was old enough to stand upright—his father had insisted on that even over his mother's complaints, and so Sean had been taught several forms of unarmed combat by a series of expert instructors—one of his Dad's Special Ops buddies even put him through the dirty fighting course!

He wasn't really afraid of a knife—especially not when it was in the hands of someone so obviously an amateur in its use. So as the slightly older man rushed him, Sean dropped into a carefully-practiced and now-reflexive sequence of moves, using an arm to block the blade while turning his body to guide it past him while driving a hip into his opponent.

Jayson stumbled and went down to one knee.

"My Dad was a Special Forces Operator," Sean told him. "He began teaching me how to fight when I was three." He kept his concentration on Jayson but spared a moment to glance at Halle who hadn't moved. "You have no training at all Jayson—and not a prayer of hurting me."

"You don't scare me! You're just a kid! And Dr. Ramnarain wants you silenced!" Jayson stood up straight and held the knife in front of him menacingly in an attempt to overawe Sean.

Sean—who was nearly a foot taller than his opponent—was not impressed. "Go home, Jayson." He gestured in the general direction of the compound. "Don't force me to hurt you!"

"You?" Jayson sneered at him. "Hurt me!" He shook his head. "Not a chance!" He closed his hand tightly around the knife's hilt and lunged at Sean's midsection

Sean saw the attempt coming from a mile away. He waited until Jayson had fully committed himself to the move, then once again slid his body out of the way while blocking the knife thrust with a downward sweep of his arm.

He didn't bother doing anything to Jayson's hurtling body—he left that to momentum and gravity—satisfying himself with a derisive laugh as his opponent fell onto his face and slid a few feet through the wet, early-morning dew.

"You bastard!" Jayson scrambled to his feet. "I'm going to gut you for that!"

"You're not going to gut me—you're not even going to touch me," Sean reset himself. "Why don't you just give up and go home?" He gestured to the watching Halle. "I'll even let you take her with you." He smiled. "If she wants to go with a helpless baby like you."

Jayson howled in rage—and launched himself at Sean once again, this time holding the knife high over his head, stabbing at his opponent's chest with all his strength.

Sean knew he couldn't keep playing with the other boy forever—however inept he might be. Eventually he'd get tired or slip in the dew-slicked grass; or perhaps Jayson would get lucky and cut him——blood flow would slow him down and weaken him until he went down.

And, of course, it was always possible that Halle might decide to get involved—that would force Sean to handle two targets at once—and one of them would be a girl.

Sean didn't fight with girls…

Weighing all that brought Sean to a decision; he couldn't afford to keep playing with Jayson—he couldn't continue to feint or duck or block the other man's blade--he had to do something to end the fight right now—while he could.

With that in mind, Sean slipped under Jayson's awkward stabbing motion and took a long step forward, slamming the flat of his right hand (he'd been taught never to use a fist—too many little bones to break) into the base of Jayson's nose.

Blood exploded in all directions as cartilage disintegrated beneath the force of the blow. Jayson cried out in pain and staggered past Sean, attack forgotten…

Sean pivoted and, as he'd been taught, brought the heel of his left foot down onto the over-extended rear of his opponent's knee.

There was a loud crack as Jayson's kneecap shattered under the force of the blow.

Screaming, the slender young man fell forward—directly onto the edge of a tombstone.

There was a loud thump, and then Jayson fell to the ground in a heap.

"Don't get up!" Sean called out as he took a long step toward his opponent. "Don't make me hurt you again."

Jayson didn't answer. He looked dazed as his head lifted from the ground. When he spotted Halle, he stretched a hand in her direction, wordlessly seeking aid...

Just before his head dropped limply into the wet grass.

"Jayson?" Halle rushed to the side of her now-motionless lover. "What's wrong?" She dropped to her knees at his side and lifted his head with both hands—then screamed in horror as she saw what had happened.

Jayson was quite dead, darkened eyes staring blankly into Halle's, the knife he tried to kill Sean with was sticking out of his gut, driven in deep when he hit the tombstone.

Sean stared at the body and thought about the things his father had taught him. The blade severed his renal artery, he nodded slowly. Put him into shock while he bled out...

That means I killed him. The realization hit Sean like a roundhouse kick. Me! I killed him as surely as if I drove the knife in myself!

"Goddamn you!" Halle charged at Sean while he stood, frozen in shock, staring at the body of the man he'd just killed. "You killed my Jayson!" She slammed into his midsection and drove him to the ground, flailing at him with both fists. "I'll kill you for that!"

Her attack saved his life.

CHAPTER FIFTEEN

That was a gunshot! Farrell broke into a run, drawing his weapon as he went. It came from ahead somewhere…

He was trying hard to remember just where Robert Piper's grave was—it had been years since he'd visited…

Just ahead, I think. He rounded a corner and slammed to a halt. He could see Sean and a young woman rolling around on the grass in front of a row of graves.

A second man—this one holding a pistol—was approaching from the direction opposite Farrell, trying hard to get a bead on one of the struggling figures.

Farrell was pretty sure he knew which one.

"Get out of the way!" The man yelled. "Give me a clear shot!"

Farrell saw the girl claw at Sean's face before attempting to roll away. She didn't quite get free before Sean slammed an elbow into her belly in an attempt to protect himself.

"Now!" She huffed out what breath was left in her. "Kill him now!"

The man raised his pistol—but Farrell had already taken aim and his target was less than ten yards away…

***

Sean barely registered the first gunshot. He was too busy keeping Halle from clawing out one of his eyes.

She fights dirty! He realized. And I don't want to fight a girl, but…

He rolled and pinned her clawed hands, then drove an elbow into her belly, trying to drive the wind—and the fight—out of her.

He didn't succeed.

""Get out of the way!" A man's voice called from behind. "Give me a clear shot!"

Halle smiled savagely—and raked the side of Sean's face with her nails. It broke his grip on her and she rolled away yelling.

"Kill him!" She came up on an elbow, snarling. "Kill him now!"

Sean turned to see who she was talking to just as two gunshots rang out, the sharp reports echoing across the monument-filled field…

***

"Sean!" Farrell rushed to the young man's side. "Are you all right?!"

"Uncle Frank?" Sean pushed himself upright, blood running down his cheek and dripping off his chin. "What…" He looked around. "Where's Halle?"

"The girl you were fighting with?" Farrell pointed to the right. "She went that way."

"Crap!" Sean got to his feet. "We've got to get her before she can reach a phone!"

"Slow down," Farrell put a hand on the youngster's shoulder. "Tell me what's going on." He nodded at the dead man lying at the very edge of the gravesite. "Who is that and why was he trying to kill you?"

Sean glanced at the body, recognition hitting as he saw the face. "He's the one who grabbed me back in New York—he said he was FBI..."

"I doubt that was the truth." Farrell left the boy and began searching the corpse, turning out pockets, checking for a wallet...

"I checked with the Feds—they had no record of you at all."

"I was at Angie's place," Sean looked at him. "That's a girl I know in New York..."

"I looked into her." Farrell grinned. "Cute—but a real piece of work."

"Yeah, took me a while to realize it but I finally figured that out." Sean looked around. "Look, we really have to get moving—if Halle manages to call Ramnarain..."

"Ramnarain?" Farrell's eyes widened. "It really is him behind this?"

"Yeah." Sean nodded. "He has a complex near here—he's been hacking into secure networks, than collecting ransoms from his victims." He looked into Farrell's eyes. "Halle and Jayson," he pointed to the second body lying among the tombstones. "Were two of his students."

"Tell me where this complex is!"

"I don't know exactly where—I mean I couldn't show it to you on a map..." Sean shook his head. "But I can lead you there!"

"That'll work." Farrell nodded toward the front of the cemetery. "My car's back there..."

"Do we just leave them here?" Sean looked at the two bodies.

"I'll call it in and get someone to pick them up..." Farrell started moving—quickly—toward his car. "CSU might find something to lead us to the 'Complex' if you can't manage it."

"I can get us there," Sean's tone was quite positive. "I'm sure of that."

"Okay," Farrell looked at him. "How many people does Ramnarain have in this 'complex'?"

"I'm not exactly sure," Sean matched the older man step for step. "Ramnarain and Waterson—they're the ones in charge, then six..." He glanced back toward Jayson's remains. "Make that five kids about my age. As for the others—cooks, guards..." He made a throwaway gesture. "I didn't have the time to make a full head count."

"I'll call in an FBI SWAT team." Farrell reached for his phone. "They can start moving while we find this complex."

"I crossed State Road 613 after I left the place—then SR 50..."

"Good for a start," he brought the phone up to his mouth and uttered two words: "Mary Max".

"Who's that?"

"My..." He smiled. "Our boss," he held the headset to his ear. "She won't like being awakened this early, but there's no help for it."

CHAPTER SIXTEEN

Mary Max, as expected, did not appreciate being awakened before dawn—but she listened carefully to what Farrell told her and promised she would dispatch a fully-armed SWAT team immediately.

"They'll be on the road in ten minutes." He pointed to the gates, just ahead. "We'll have to find the place and vector them in." He looked at Sean. "You're sure you can do that?"

"Let's go." Sean clambered over the fence, dropping onto the gravel without apparent effort. "We've got to get to them before they can clear out."

"Okay," Farrell joined the youngster, not quite as gracefully, and led him to the car. "Which way?"

Sean guided the car around the cemetery and onto the road he'd paralleled for most of his journey. "About eight miles this way," he pointed forward. "Do you have a laptop or a phone with internet capability I can use?"

"Here," Farrell handed the boy his own phone. "What do you have in mind?"

"The complex has its own Wi-Fi set-up. If I can hack into it…"

"Wouldn't you have to be closer?"

"Maybe not." Sean turned the I-Phone on its side and began working the keyboard. "If I can find Halle's phone, I can use it to leapfrog forward…"

"You're assuming she's still around here?"

"Even if she has a car," Sean looked ahead. "She can't be too far ahead of us."

Halle, they soon decided, was nowhere in the area—either that or she had been aware of the possibility of Sean hacking her and turned her phone off to keep him from doing so. Whichever it was, Sean was unsuccessful in his attempt to hack into the Wi-Fi in question and was forced to satisfy himself with guiding Farrell down a series of roads until a familiar edifice came into sight.

"Stop near here," Sean pointed at the half-concealed shack that he knew held the doorway to the complex's emergency exit. "They're right under that."

"Right," Farrell took the phone back from the youngster and texted co-ordinates to the FBI team. When he was sure it had gotten through, he gave the phone back to Sean. "Think you can hack into their system now?"

"Unless they've shut it down…" Sean searched for a Wi-Fi source—found several—and started the process of eliminating those that wouldn't help. He was almost done when a massive explosion erupted in the field beyond the hidden door…

***

"Not much left," the sun was nearly at zenith by the time the FBI team finished their examination of the complex. "It looks as if they had explosive charges preset and when they were sure that we knew where they were…" He raised his hands in an explosive gesture.

"No bodies—so they got out safely." He looked at the FBI man. "Did you find any computers? Servers, storage units? Anything that might give us a lead?"

"I didn't see anything down there that was even close to being intact—but CSU is in there now, if there's anything left, they'll find it."

"Thanks," Farrell nodded. "I appreciate the effort."

"Do you know this was one of our facilities?" The FBI agent asked.

"What do you mean?"

"In the fifties the federal government built several emergency complexes in which officials could seek refuge in the case of a nuclear war or," the agent smiled. "Something of that nature."

"I heard about Greenbrier Resort." Sean put in. "The resort hotel in White Sulphur Springs, West Virginia…"

"That one was for the really big shots." The agent gestured at the crater behind them. "This one was for bureaucrats and minor officials."

"Bastard is using our own resources against us!" Farrell gestured to Sean to join him and headed back to the car. "I've got to get back to my office and make a bunch of phone calls."

"Make one right now," Sean asked him.

"Hmmm?"

"Put a guard on my Mom and Sister—I'm sure Halle will try to hurt them if she can find a way."

"Good idea," Farrell picked up his phone. "I'll get someone on post right now." He looked at Sean. "Do you want to go home and join them?"

"Hell no!" he shook his head. "I want to see this through." He looked Farrell in the eye. "Those people have my computer—they might use one of my programs to hurt someone." He sucked at his lower lip. "I can't just sit back and let that happen."

"Okay," Farrell started the car. "From this point on, you're my partner—you handle the computer stuff and I'll handle the gunplay." He glanced at Sean. "Okay?"

"Okay." Sean grinned. "I'm not all that good with a handgun anyway."

"Really," Farrell got onto the road and gunned it. "Your Dad told a different story…"

"He exaggerated," Sean shrugged. "I'm nowhere as good as he said."

"Once we get finished with the briefings and get everything else sorted and under way, you can show me—there's a range right in the basement of the FBI building."

"Okay," Sean sat back. "But I'm telling you the truth—I'm not that good."

"I hope you're good enough to pass the FBI's firearm test." He raised an eyebrow. "I wouldn't want to take you into the field unarmed." He grinned. "You've got to be able to watch my six!"

"You want me to carry a gun?"

"I want you to be ready if you come up against someone else with a gun." He turned onto I-95 and increased speed. "I don't want to have to do your shooting for you."

"Dad always told me that when he worked with you, that was his job."

"Sometimes," Farrell smiled. "Sometimes one of my drones did the shooting for him."

"Drones?"

"I'll tell you all about it someday," Farrell took the turnoff onto the Fourteenth Street Bridge. "But not right now—we have other things to discuss."

"Like Dr. Ramnarain?"

"And his merry band." They drove past the old Treasury Building. "You'll have to describe them for me so I can find out who they are."

"It's too bad," Sean replied. "Most of them seemed like nice kids…"

CHAPTER SEVENTEEN

UNKNOWN LOCATION #2--
NORTHEASTERN VIRGINIA

"I had to leave almost all of my clothes behind!" Carole complained. "It's not fair!"

"If you hadn't left them, you'd be dead or in jail by now." Mike told her. "And you still have plenty of things to wear."

"And, just in case you don't have enough…" Ramnarain had been passing the couple's room just in time to hear Carole's lament. "There're lots of stores in this area—it'll be easy for you to replace anything that was lost." He looked at the two. "You didn't leave anything that would identify you, did you? I'm not sure just how effective our explosives were—some of the charges were quite old."

Carole shrugged. "I bought most of my stuff at thrift shops—it's not as if they had fancy labels or anything."

"Good," Ramnarain nodded. "Finish unpacking what you did save and join me in the Common Room—we have to make some plans." His eyes darkened. "Payback for all the trouble Mr. Piper and his friends caused us."

"It was all Sean's fault," Mike put in. "If he hadn't gotten out …"

"I sent people to take care of Sean." Ramnarain stroked his chin. "I should hear back from them soon."

131

"Good." Mike nodded. "He was too much of a goody-goody for us anyway!"

"Not to mention the fact..." Carole put in, grinning. "That he beat you pretty bad when the two of you played 'Call of Duty'."

"He did not!" Mike snarled. "I let him win just to make him feel welcome."

"Right!" Carole sneered. "You let him win!"

Ramnarain left them to their bickering and headed for his office—he was becoming concerned about Jayson and Halle.

They should have gotten in touch by now. He settled into his new, rather stiff, seat and clicked the brand new laptop on the desk 'ON'. I hope nothing has happened to them—those two would be very hard to replace...

***

J. EDGAR HOOVER BUILDING— WASHINGTON D.C.

"His name is Jayson Harding," Sean stared at the photo on the screen in front of him as he listened to the background briefing. "He was born in Philadelphia and raised by his Mother and Grandmother after his father disappeared."

The FBI briefer brought up another image—a mug shot.

"At fourteen, he got mixed up with a local gang. His grades dropped and he was picked up several times for various petty crimes." The briefer looked at Sean and Farrell. "As he was a juvenile and the Philly PD had no room in Juvie, none of the

132

charges stuck—the state kept sending him back to Mom."

"How did he get into college?"

"During one of his infrequent visits to High School, one of his teachers discovered that young Jayson had a real talent for Math—she encouraged him to use those talents, eventually, getting him to the 'Math Olympic'" The briefer looked at Sean. "Jayson did very well—won several of them. The experience got him back into school and encouraged, his teachers got the school board to give him a used computer…"

The image changed.

"His grades skyrocketed and, for a time, it appeared that he would be a real inner-city success story." The Briefer shook his head. "Right up until the moment his Dad came back into the picture."

Another mug shot—this one of a teen-aged Jayson. "Dad listened to all the stories about Jayson's skill with math and the computer—then got the boy involved in white-collar crime— computer hacking; identity theft; spoofing ATMs— that kind of thing." The briefer shook his head. "It appears that 'Dad' kept all of the money that came out of those schemes."

Another image appeared—this one of Jayson in a courthouse. "When he was finally found and arrested, he had just turned eighteen—old enough to be charged as an adult. He had no defense at the trial—his Father had left him holding the very empty bag—and the judge was ready to send him to prison for a very long time…"

A new image—Ramnarain's image—appeared.

"That's when Dr. Gerald Ramnarain intervened. The good doctor was, at that time, a Senior Professor of Computer Science at Rutgers University. He had a DOD grant to train gifted youngsters in high-level computer science." He looked at Sean. "His trainees were to be the next generation of Homeland Security Operatives—a group of 'Cyber Cops', if you will."

"What happened?" Farrell asked.

"The judge gave Jayson to Ramnarain with the understanding that he be trained to use his talents in a good cause." The FBI man shrugged. "Apparently that didn't work out very well."

"What changed Ramnarain?" Farrell put in.

"He lost his University position—something about one of his students hacking into various departmental databases." The FBI man shrugged. "That loss came at about the same time his grant money from Homeland Security ran out. He applied for a new grant to keep his program going." A grant form appeared on the screen. "It was turned down without comment—and the money went to a different scientist," the agent shook his head. "One whose Father-in-Law was on the grant committee."

"That's all it took to turn Ramnarain rogue?"

"It's all we've been able to find so far." The agent turned the projector off and brought up the lights. "Ramnarain disappeared a few months later—at the time we assumed he left the University to go into private business." The agent frowned. "It appears we may have underestimated him."

"What about his partner?" Sean asked.

"Partner?" The FBI man turned to him. "We don't know about any partners!"

"He was clearly working with a Ms. Waterson. It seemed to me that she was the one making all the big, non-science decisions."

"Waterson..." The FBI man thought for a long moment. "That name sounds vaguely familiar."

"Forty to forty five years old, five foot six or seven, blond hair, blue eyes..."

"Describes about twenty-five percent of the female population of this country."

"She had a very precise way of talking..." Sean noted. "I've only heard a few people talk that way in my life. I would bet that she was in some sort of government service position."

"Waterson..." The agent made a note on his tablet. "We'll run the name and description and see what we come up with." He looked at Sean. "You're sure you don't know what their next target might be?"

"Nobody told me anything—I hadn't been 'accepted' yet." Sean bit his lip, thinking. "I did see something when I hacked into their security system—a file name—nothing more..."

"What was the name?" Farrell asked.

"Operation Hemo." Sean told him. "That's all I saw."

"What the hell does that mean?" The FBI agent put in.

"Could be anything," Farrell glanced at his watch. "And we don't have time to deal with it right now." He turned to the FBI man. "Go and check out this Waterson woman—I have a meeting with CIA and some others later this morning—I want you to join us. We've got to find a way to locate this crew before they try something else."

"What time?" The agent asked.

"Eleven—meeting room two."

"I'll be there." The man stood up, nodded toward Sean. "Nice work, young man. Without you, we'd have no idea who was behind those attacks."

"He's right, Sean." Farrell smiled when the FBI man left. "You did the right thing sneaking out and contacting me."

"Maybe," Sean shook his head. "But it might have been better if I had stayed and found out where their next strike was going. Besides..." He turned to stare at the wall where Jayson's dead eyes stared back. "If I had stayed, I might not have been forced to kill Jayson..."

"It wasn't your fault. He attacked you!"

"Yeah." Sean shrugged. "But I keep seeing him—and Halle--glaring at me—hating me." He looked at Farrell. "Uncle Frank, I watched him die—right in front of me! I saw the knife, saw the blood..."

"You can't undo that," Farrell slapped him on the back. "So you have to find a way to deal with it." He looked into the youngster's face. "That kind of thing is always going to be part of the job."

"The job..."

"Ramnarain and his acolytes are going to kill a lot of innocent people if we don't stop them." He looked at Sean, raising an eyebrow. "You're going to have to ask yourself if that's important enough to spill their blood if that's wat you have to do to stop them."

Sean didn't answer—he just stared at the wall—and into the depths of his own wounded and confused soul...

CHAPTER EIGHTEEN

UNKNOWN LOCATION #2-
NORTHEASTERN VIRGINIA

"Where have you been?" Ramnarain asked when Halle appeared in his office the next morning. "And where's Jayson?"

"Jayson's dead!" She snarled. "Killed by that bastard, Piper!"

"Slow down." Ramnarain held up a hand. "Tell me everything…"

"It took us a while to find any sign of him," the girl told the older man. "The tracker didn't tell us anything at first so we began to think he'd managed to hitch a ride and had gone beyond the range of the thing—maybe already reached a town or city," she looked at him. "I wanted to come home and report but Jayson and Grant wanted to keep looking."

"It took a while but the tracker finally gave us a signal—one that led us to a large, walled-in area…" Her mouth twitched as she suppressed a sob. "We should have come home…"

"This wall!" Ramnarain kept his tone light and professional. "What was special about it?"

"We played a light across it—just in case Piper was hiding on top and Jayson saw something…" Her mouth went tight. "We got out and moved in for a closer look…" She looked into Ramnarain's eyes. "The mortar between some of the blocks in the wall had been disturbed—as if someone had climbed over." She nodded slowly. "The tracker

agreed—it pointed to the other side of the wall."
She shrugged. "So Grant took the car and drove
around to the parking area while Jayson and I
climbed over the wall…"

"Parking area?"

"Yeah," Halle nodded. "The wall was the one
around Arlington National Cemetery."

"What was Sean doing there?"

"When I found him, he said that he was visiting
his father." Halle stared at the wall. "Said that he
needed to talk things over with him."

"His father was there?" Ramnarain frowned. "I
thought…"

"It was his father's grave." Halle licked dry
lips. "Sean had just reached it when we got there."

"And?"

"I told him that we had decided that he couldn't
be trusted. Told him that you had ordered him
silenced." Her eyes clouded over. "Jayson didn't
wait for Grant to catch up—he just pulled his knife
and went right at the kid."

"And?"

"Piper beat him—flipped him over so he landed
on his own knife. I saw …" Tears began to flow
down her cheeks. "I saw him die."

"Afterwards?"

"I wasn't really thinking straight—I should
have just held him there—talked to him until Grant
arrived." She looked at Ramnarain. "But I couldn't
do that. I had to…"

"I understand, Halle. You attacked him?"

"Yes. I tried to claw his eyes out—rip out his
throat." She stared at the wall. "He didn't want to
fight me—he just kept blocking me until…"

"Until?"

"Grant finally got there. He told me to get out of the way—out of his line of fire."

"Did you?"

"I tried—but there somebody else showed up—somebody who fired before Grant did."

"Mr. Grant is dead?"

"Yeah," Halle nodded. "I ran before they could get me too—ran to the car and drove away just as fast as I could." She looked at Ramnarain. "They didn't follow me here—I'm sure of that!"

"Why didn't you call?"

"I was afraid that Piper might hack my phone so I powered it down..."

"That was wise." Ramnarain stepped to her side and put a fatherly arm across her shoulder. "Very wise indeed."

"We've got to kill him!" Her hate-filled eyes looked into his. "We've got to!"

"He's no doubt contacted the FBI or some other Federal agency by now." Ramnarain told her. "He'll be heavily guarded."

"We have to do something! Jayson has to be avenged!"

"We will certainly do something." Ramnarain put his hands on her upper arms and turned her so she was looking straight at him. "I want you to get all the information about his family you can find. If there's a way for us to get at his mother and sister..." A nasty smile crossed the scientist's lips. "That would hurt him far more than anything else I can think of doing."

Halle nodded.

139

"While you are doing that, the rest of us will initiate phase two." He raised an eyebrow at her look. "It will be harder without you and Jayson—but I think we can handle it."

"All right," Halle nodded. "I'll look for a way to get back at the bastard." She looked at the older man. "But I want to be there when it happens—I want to see his face!"

"I think we can arrange that," the Professor nodded. "Now, find your new room and get some rest. I want to begin implementing Phase Two before noon tomorrow."

Halle nodded and stood, hesitating for a second, eyes on the Professor. "Remember, I have to be there when he dies!"

"You will be, Halle." Ramnarain told her. "You have my word."

***

J.EDGAR HOOVER BUILDING— WASHINGTON D.C.

"I thought you said you couldn't shoot!" Farrell said as he examined Sean's target.

"I said I wasn't all that good with a handgun," the youngster replied. "I'm okay with a rifle."

"Sean," Farrell held up the target. "Every round is in the black…"

"Yeah," Sean spread three fingers over the pattern. "But the pattern's not tight—and that last shot…" He pointed at a hole in the upper right-hand portion of the black. "It almost missed!"

Farrell shook his head.

"Dad would have put all six rounds dead in the center of the target—and you'd have been able to cover them with a quarter!"

"Your dad was one of the best shots I ever met," Farrell agreed. "And you're not too far behind him!" He gestured to the Glock 9mm Sean had used. "What do you think of the Glock?"

"It's a nice pistol," Sean smiled. "Good balance, points well…"

"Good," Farrell looked at his charge. "Put it in the locker over there—take the key with you—we'll find you a holster later—right now, we have a meeting to attend."

"You want me to carry this?" Sean lifted the Glock, ejected the magazine and the round in the chamber, checked the safety, and placed everything in the locker indicated.

"Yeah," Farrell smiled. "You're my partner—at least until this thing is over." He looked at his watch. "And that means you get to come to all the meetings I have to go to!"

***

The meeting in question was held in a small room on the eighth floor of the Northwest E- Street side of the FBI building. The range was on the Pennsylvania Avenue side which meant Sean and Farrell had to hurry through the open-air courtyard that connected the two to reach the meeting.

"Wow," Sean frowned as he saw the cracks in the crumbling concrete that formed the exterior walls. "That doesn't look too sturdy!"

"Building's obsolete," Farrell told him. "It was badly designed to begin with and now…" He shook his head. "They'll build a new one—eventually but

141

right now the money just isn't there." He grinned. "They have more important things to spend it on— Climate Change, Solyndra, stuff like that!"

They hurried through the doors and, beyond them, a metal detector manned by an elderly uniformed officer who nodded when Farrell produced his badge and vouched for Sean.

"Elevator's over there," Farrell pointed, as he glanced at a just-received text on his cell phone. "Mary Max says they're about to start."

Mary Max, Sean discovered when the two of them entered the conference room, was Mary Max Halston—Farrell's boss, friend, and confidant. As the senior officer present she sat at the head of the table with a handful of secretaries and aides against the wall behind her.

To her right were three FBI agents. Sean recognized one of them as the man who'd led the SWAT team tasked with assaulting Ramnarain's compound early that morning.

Opposite them—on Mary Max's left—were representatives of several other government organizations—including the FAA and NTSB.

"Who is this, Mr. Farrell?" Mary Max asked as soon as he and Sean found seats.

"This is Sean Piper," he nodded to the young man next to him. "He was the one who located the source of the recent cyber-attack on transport in New York."

Mary Max nodded at Sean, then gestured toward the FBI people on her left. "You may begin the briefing."

"Yes, Ma'am." The senior FBI agent nodded before gesturing to an assistant along the back wall of the room. "Go ahead."

"CSU has confirmed," the assistant began. "That the hacks that penetrated both the FAA system in Islip and the NY Subway system in Manhattan originated at the compound we raided this morning."

The senior FBI agent leaned forward and broke in: "We were able to make that determination by a careful examination of the entry codes they used." He looked around the table. "An entry code that should not exist—but somehow did and was in their possession."

"The code was hardwired into the computer system at the facility in question," the third agent picked up. "That system, designed and installed in 1959, was ordered modernized and refitted less than a year ago."

"By who?" Mary Max asked.

"By the National Security Agency." The senior agent answered. "The place is...was..." He shrugged. "Was designed and built to be a National Security Bunker," he looked around the room. "All such facilities were originally built with a direct connection..." He looked at the faces around him. "And I do mean a direct connection—no interfaces, no Wi-Fi, no dial up—a direct cable connection to the 'National Science Foundation Network'." He smiled at the questions in the faces around him. "That was one of the early versions of what has since become more popularly known as: 'the internet'."

"The NSFN," the first briefer continued. "Was decommissioned in 1995." He raised an eyebrow. "This discovery proves that connections to the system were, for some reason, left in place and, as a result, the bunkers are a perfect place for hackers to gain access to the World Wide Web." He shrugged. "From a place that can't be tracked or blocked."

"You said bunkers—plural," Mary Max looked at him. "There are more?"

"Initial research indicates that at least eight more such 'bunkers' exist within the Continental United States." The senior FBI man looked at his notes. "We're trying to determine their locations as we speak."

"The FBI doesn't know where they are?" Mary Max asked.

"They…" the FBI man shrugged. "They dropped off the radar more than twenty years ago. We had no idea any of them were still serviceable…"

"Who would know?"

"The General Services Administration is in charge of that kind of thing," one of the officials said. "But as this was built for a war emergency, it might fall under the military's purview…"

"So you're telling me that no one knows?" Mary Max looked around the table. When she got no response, she turned to one of the assistants seated against the wall. "Find out for me, will you John?"

"Yes, Ma'am," 'John' replied as he hurried out of the conference room.

"Now," Mary Max turned to Farrell. "What do you have, Frank?"

"Sean here says he saw a file that he believes held the plan for a new attack—but he didn't have time to study it…"

"Operation Hemo," the FBI agent who'd been with them the night before interjected. "That's what he called it."

"Look into the terminology," Mary Max instructed a second assistant seated against the wall. "Find out what it could possibly stand for."

That man nodded—and hurried out of the room.

"Anything else?"

"Ramnarain is using young people to write his code and do his dirty work." Farrell noted, glancing at Sean. "He tells them he's after money—but I'm not so sure…"

"What do we know of this Dr. Ramnarain?"

"My people are doing a complete background check right now," the senior FBI agent told her. "We know he was a Professor at Rutgers University. We know he led a Government training program designed to produce high-level computer experts…"

"And we know that he lost the funding for that program due to governmental nepotism." Farrell added. "I don't know enough about him to say that was enough to get him angry enough to be willing to kill innocent people…"

"If there's anything else," the FBI man asserted. "We'll find it."

"Quickly," Farrell told him. "I don't think we have much time."

"Why do you say that?" Mary Max asked.

"We just smashed his headquarters and killed two of his people." Farrell ran his eyes across the other men and women around the table. "He's going to have to do something soon—if only to show his own crew that he hasn't lost control."

"You think he'll perpetrate another attack?"

"I'm sure of it." Farrell nodded. "And it'll be soon." He rubbed his cheek. "Very soon."

"All right," Mary Max nodded. "Everyone has something to look into." She glanced at her watch. "We meet back here in six hours." Her eyes burned into the FBI agent. "Please make sure you have something for us by then." She stood. "Farrell—I want to see you in my office." She glanced at Sean. "Bring your young friend."

Then she was gone—and the meeting dissolved into a series of hasty conversations.

***

"I take it you want this young man," Mary Max stared at Sean, eyes searching. "To be your partner while we work this case?"

"He's already been read in. He volunteered to help us—and you know that I wanted him recruited, Hell..." Farrell shrugged. "His computer skills are way beyond mine." He smiled. "And you should see him shoot!"

"How old is he?"

"Eighteen Ma'am," Sean gave her his most solemn look. "My birthday was in November."

"I don't know..."

Sean leaned forward, eyes serious. "My father was only eighteen when he joined the Army..."

"Forget about how old he is—it doesn't matter," Farrell leaned forward, looked at his

146

superior. "He's the one who led us to the hackers' compound and told us who they were…"

"And was forced to kill another young man in a knife fight!" Mary Max retorted.

"I didn't have a knife, Ma'am." Sean looked down at the floor. "And I didn't mean to kill him."

"We discussed this. Sean's father taught him a lot of things before he went on that last mission," Farrell's eyes burned into those of the woman behind the desk. "You recall what I told you about that…"

"I am aware of the fact that we owe his family a debt—as you've been quick to point out more than once." Mary Max looked at Sean, looked at Farrell, looked back at Sean—and shrugged. "Make sure he's properly entered on the rolls—from the day you first recruited him." She caught Farrell in her glare. "Give him the appropriate salary…" The glare intensified. "And don't you dare let him get hurt!"

"I wouldn't think of it." Farrell nodded. "Thanks."

"Now get out there and find where those bastards have gone to ground! We've got to stop them before they act again!"

None of them knew it yet, but it was already far too late for that…

CHAPTER NINETEEN

"Michael? Carole?" Ramnarain stepped up to look over the young couple's shoulder. "Are you ready?"

"We've gained access to the net," Mike told him. "Our address should be unreadable so nobody will be able to backtrack it..."

"I'm searching for an appropriate aircraft," Carole glanced at her mentor. "It might take a few minutes."

"There's no rush." Ramnarain patted her on the shoulder. "Just make sure you don't make any mistakes."

"I don't think that'll be too difficult," she smiled at the professor. "We've been running simulations on this one for quite a while!"

"Good," Ramnarain turned toward his office. "Notify me when you've started the procedure." He called back over his shoulder. "I want to watch."

***

ON FINAL APPROACH TO REAGAN AIRPORT

Captain Howard Berlinski sighed as he closed his hands over the yoke of the Boeing 757 and flipped the auto-pilot to 'OFF'.

"Not too crowded today," Louis James, his co-pilot remarked as they continued their measured descent into Washington's 'Reagan' Airport.

"I hate this place," Berlinski trimmed the wing flaps. "The river's too close and there's lots of 'restricted' airspace on all sides."

"Don't worry," James smiled. "Nobody's going to shoot us down."

"I hope you're right." Berlinski matched his friend's smile. "Because I have a hot date tonight!"

"You still seeing that girl from the State Department?"

"Yup," Berlinski smiled. "And if all goes well, I might..." He gripped the yoke harder. "Something's wrong!"

"What is it?"

"I don't know..." Berlinski pulled back on the wheel again. "The Yoke won't move!" He glanced at the instrument panel. "Check the auto-pilot! Maybe..."

"Autopilot is off." James leaned forward, studying the instrument panel. "Everything looks good!"

"Try your yoke—see if you can move it!"

"Okay..." The other man took a long moment to struggle with his wheel—to no avail. "You're right—it won't move at all." He looked at the Captain. "What do we do?"

"You call Air Traffic Control—declare an emergency—get us some room!"

"Roger."

"I'll see if I can free the controls..." Berlinski yanked hard, shook the wheel. "If it's just mechanical..."

"Washington control, this is Jet Blue 895." He watched his companion fight with the wheel for a moment, then sighed and went on: "Mayday—I say

149

again, Mayday! Jet Blue 895 is experiencing control problems! Mayday! Mayday!"

The yoke suddenly moved—in the direction opposite the pilot's struggle—sliding all the way forward.

"It's got us in a dive!" Berlinski pulled back with all his might. "I can't get any control! We're gonna…"

The two men were still struggling with the controls when Jet Blue Flight 895 rolled over and dove toward the center of the city.

***

'Union Station,' Gene read from the brochure he had taken at the entrance to the building. "Is one of Washington D.C.'s busiest and best-known places to visit. It features many shops, cafes, and restaurants…" He looked at the girl with him. "I told you we could find something to eat here!"

"This city is full of all kinds of exotic restaurants!" Mary was younger than Gene—and not a train enthusiast. "Why did we come to a Railroad Station?"

"I haven't seen this place since I was a kid," he answered. "It was so beautiful then…"

"It's still pretty," Mary looked around. "Although I think it's odd that the skylights don't let in any sunlight."

"That's because," he held up the brochure. "They're blocked by a new sub-roof they built to support the upper structure of the building…" He looked around. "What's that noise?"

"What noise?" She glanced in his direction. "All I can hear is people arguing…" She frowned.

"Although, now that I think about it, there is a kind of whistling sound…"

"That's it!" He looked up at the glossy white ceiling. "It's coming from above. I wonder what it could be…"

His eyes widened in shock as he saw the ceiling begin to collapse over his head. He tried to push Mary out of the way…

It was far too late. They were both crushed beneath flaming ruins as the runaway airliner smashed into the central concourse…

***

"What was that?" Sean frowned as the FBI building trembled around him.

"I don't know." Farrell handed his partner the holster he'd just signed for. "Put this on and let's find out what's happening."

They found out as soon as they left the building.

"That…" Farrell stared at a towering pillar of smoke and flame just a few blocks up the street. "That has to be Union Station!"

"A train crash couldn't cause that!" Sean shook his head. "It's got to be something else!"

"A bomb maybe…" Farrell shook himself. "Come on," he put a hand on Sean's shoulder and led him to the entrance of the taller half of the bifurcated building. "We can get more information inside then we can anywhere else!"

***

"Are you sure?"

Mary Max was on the phone when Farrell barged into her office with Sean was less than a step behind.

She signaled them to wait.

"What did they say?" She listened intently. "Nothing else?" She shook her head. "Get me all the information you can—I already have a meeting scheduled."

She clicked the phone off and looked at Farrell. "An airliner enroute to Reagan lost control and vectored into Union Station." Her eyes were bleak as they looked into his. "The pilots sent out a 'Mayday' a few moments before the crash. They reported that their controls were locked."

"Ramnarain." Farrell bit his lip. "It has to be Ramnarain."

"But why?"

"A demonstration of power." Farrell stepped to the front of Mary Max's desk and leaned forward, looking her in the eye. "We chased him out of his stronghold—this is his way of showing us that he can still hurt us."

"What can we do?"

"You've got to get the overall threat level raised—I can't be sure without looking at the black box data but it's possible they could have crashed that plane wherever they wanted—the Capital, the White House..." He looked into her eyes. "Anywhere."

"I'll talk to the Director immediately..."

"Tell him he has to ground all flights until we get this sorted out."

"Farrell! Do you know what that would do to this country?"

"It'd save lives." He stared at her. "Isn't that what we're here for?"

She sighed. "I'll talk to him. You make sure that the two of you are both here for the meeting this afternoon. We've got to find these people and shut them down." Her jaw tightened. "And we've got to do it before they do anything else!"

CHAPTER TWENTY

UNKNOWN LOCATION #2-
NORTHEASTERN VIRGINIA

"You said they were still renovating the station," Carole said as she and the others watched the television coverage of the plane crash. "You said we could keep the casualties to a minimum."

"I was mistaken," Ramnarain told her, putting a calming hand on her shoulder. "I thought…"

"Those renovations were finished more than twenty years ago!" Carole shoved his hand away and glared at him. "Don't lie to me!"

"I'm sorry…"

"I'm not a child." Carole's eyes bored into Ramnarain's. "I don't care if people get killed—I just care about getting paid." She raised an eyebrow. "You'd better make sure we get paid off for this one—understand?"

"I give you my word," Ramnarain gave her a bow. "You will get your money."

"Good," Carole smiled. "Now, what's the next target?"

***

FINAL APPROACH TO LOS ANGELES
INTERNATIONAL

United Airlines Flight 703 had just started its descent to Lax when things started to go wrong.

"What's wrong with the yoke?" First Officer Monica Lewin blurted, fighting with the wheel which, despite her best efforts, would not move.

"What do you mean?" Captain Macintosh had over four thousand hours in the Boeing 757 and thought he knew everything there was to know about the aircraft.

"See if you can get her level," Lewin told him. "Maybe the problem's with my controls."

"Okay," Macintosh flipped the switch that transferred control from the co-pilot's position to his own.

Immediately, the control yoke locked into place.

"That's odd." The captain looked over the board, searching for any anomalous indications. "Is the autopilot off?"

"That's what it says," Lewin touched the indicated switch. "Switch is in the 'OFF' position."

"Call LAX," the captain touched the throttles, gave the plane a little more power. "Tell them that we have a problem and that we're going to overfly them while we check it out." He rattled the yoke, trying to loosen it by sheer muscle power. "I'd rather be over water while we handle a problem like this."

"Roger that," Lewin flicked her radio to LAX traffic control and began repeating the Captain's message.

She never finished.

"Shit!"

The Captain's curse snapped her off in mid-report.

"What's wrong?"

155

"Look at the angle of attack!" He fought with the yoke, added more power. "We're going down!"

"Can't you..."

"Nothing's working!" He yelled in frustration. "I can't get it under control!"

Lewin added her strength to his, trying—without effect—to get the aircraft level.

It's not working!" Macintosh gave her an anguished look. "Call it in!"

"Mayday! Mayday!" Lewin did her best to keep her voice even. "This is United Flight 703 out of New York reporting an emergency..."

"Roger seven-zero-three," came the very prompt reply. "What seems to be the problem?"

"We have lost control of the aircraft," she looked at the altimeter. "We are losing altitude at a rate of..." Her breath caught as the truth became clear. "Nearly five hundred feet a minute."

"Roger seven-zero-three," the controller's voice roughened as he realized that this meant. "Can you make it to LAX?"

"I don't know..." She looked at Macintosh who gave a quick negative shake of the head. "The Captain says that's a negative."

"Roger," she could hear several voices in the background as controllers and supervisors rushed to offer what help they could. "Hold one..."

"Roger that." Lewin watched the ground come up beneath her. That's the city over there; she could see the mass of buildings crisscrossed by freeways full of cars. That means we're about forty or so miles from the airport... She did some math in her head. We're not going to make it!

"United seven-zero-three, LA control asks if you want to try to land at Long Beach—it's closer and on your line of flight."

"What do you think, Mike?" She asked Macintosh.

"I don't know," sweat was beading his forehead now. "If we had even a little control..."

Lewin nodded—and got back on the radio. "LA control, pilot advises that we don't have enough control to attempt landing at Long Beach." She looked at her partner. "We will attempt to get out over water..."

"Roger, United seven-zero-three. Radar shows you thirty miles from LAX..." There was another long pause. "Is there anything we can do?"

"Pray for us, LA control." Lewin swallowed hard. "We're gonna need it."

***

J. EDGAR HOOVER BUILDING—
WASHINGTON D.C.

"This happened less than ten minutes ago," Mary Max announced when the evening meeting started. This time, there was a Deputy Director sitting on the FBI side of the table and a senior White House advisor sitting opposite him—both were staring at the big-screen TV on the far wall—and the picture on it.

"That is United Flight Seven Oh Three." Mary Max kept silent as the screen showed the jet smashing into the very edge of the four-oh-five Freeway before cartwheeling across the road AND smashing into a hotel before exploding into flaming ruin. "It reported loss of control while on approach to LAX." She sighed. "The pilots were trying to get her to the ocean." She nodded toward the screen. "They didn't quite make it."

"I thought we requested all flights be pancaked?" Farrell asked.

"The White House wouldn't give the order," Mary Max told him. "Said it would be 'too big a hit to the recovering economy.'"

"And what's this?" He pointed at the huge fire raging on the television. "Is that going to help the economy?"

"Frank…"

"Come on, Mary Max—you know as well as I do that it's going to happen again unless we do something—right now!."

"I…" Sean looked around as all eyes turned to him. "I think I might have an idea…" He set his jaw and looked at Mary Max. "What kind of plane was that?" He nodded toward the screen.

"What do you mean?"

"Was it a Boeing 757?"

"I don't know." She turned to one of her assistants. "Find out." Her eyes came back to Sean. "What are you thinking?"

"The plane that crashed into Union Station earlier today was a Boeing 757. If this new crash was the same kind of plane…" He looked at Mary Max and shrugged. "It's possible that Ramnarain and the others have found a fault in the plane's control structure—a way they can get into the fly-by-wire system and override it…"

"Like that hacker who said he got control of the thrusters on several aircraft..." The White House aide muttered.

"I thought that was debunked," the sole CIA agent at the table said. "Both Boeing and Airbus said it was too complicated..."

"Gentlemen," Mary Max held up a hand for silence, than looked at Sean. "Do you have any proof of this, Mr. Piper?"

"No Ma'am," he shook his head. "We'll have to look through the plane's wreckage to find proof..."

"Ms. Halston?" The assistant broke in. "NTSB says the plane in Los Angeles was a Boeing 757—just like the one in Washington."

"Thank you, Will." Mary Max thought for a long moment, then: "Mr. Piper, I want you to do whatever you can to check out your theory—I will instruct the NTSB to co-operate with you in any way possible."

"Yes Ma'am."

"Now..."

"Ms. Halston!" An aide came rushing in from outside. "We have a communication from some people who say they caused the crash." He passed a piece of paper to her. "They have demands..."

"They'll want money." Farrell said. "A lot of money."

"What makes you say that, Mr. Farrell?" The White House advisor—a Ms. Dizon asked.

"We don't know what Dr. Ramnarain really wants," he looked around the table. "But we do know that his working force—the young people who do the actual hacking for him—are in it for the money." He nodded at Sean. "My associate here was offered a substantial salary to join them—and I don't see any other way for them to 'earn' any cash if they don't make such demands…"

"You're partially right," Mary Max, face pale, held up the piece of paper she'd been given. "Dr. Ramnarain demands that we pay him fifty million dollars in diamonds within twenty-four hours," she looked around the table. "If we don't pay, he says he will cause another crash every hour thereafter until we comply."

"Can we get the White House to ground all flights now?" Farrell asked.

"I don't know," Mary Max shook her head and looked at Ms. Dizon. "What do you think, Steff?"

"I'm not sure…" Ms. Dizon looked down at the table, thinking. "The President was hoping we'd learn something useful from the black box but now…" She sighed and turned to her own assistant, seated directly behind her. "How many planes are in the air right now?" She asked him.

The man worked on his laptop for a few seconds, then looked at her. "I can put it on the big screen."

"Do it."

"Here's a satellite view of the US—you can see the radar traces of all the civilian planes currently in the air…"

There was a gasp from the collected officials and aides—the air was so full of markers they appeared to be a solid mass.

"As near as I can determine," the aide continued. "There are nearly seven thousand planes in the air over the United States at this exact moment."

"Seven thousand…" Ms. Dizon muttered. "We'll have to pay."

"I don't think we can," Mary Max told her. "They want something besides the money." Her eyes moved to the far side of the table. "They want Sean Piper."

CHAPTER TWENTY-ONE

US MARINES CORPS STORAGE DEPOT
QUANTICO VIRGINIA

Gunnery Sergeant John H. Crews was bored. It's such a waste of my time, he told himself. We're never going to use these damned weapons again!

He cursed the luck that had brought him to this place and this position. Assigned as Sergeant of the Guard at Marine Depot Foxtrot, he thought. Quite a comedown from my previous assignment!

Crews had been in Marine Recon and had seen action in both Iraq and Afghanistan. It wasn't until he'd rotated stateside that he'd gotten into trouble.

Too many women, he couldn't help but smile. And too much---way too much--to drink!

Crews had always been attracted to the wrong kind of woman—this time, it had cost him.

It wasn't as if I was going to let her keep my rifle, he thought. I just brought it into the apartment so I wouldn't have to leave it sitting in the trunk of my car...

The MP's had understood that—but they couldn't just let things go. After all, the girl had emptied the weapon's magazine into an ex-boyfriend's car!

That meant Crews—who they found passed out drunk in the girl's apartment—got arrested and, even with a very kind and generous CO who opted for administrative punishment instead of a court martial, had lost a stripe and his spot in Recon.

It was a miracle that they hadn't pulled his security clearance.

Which is the only reason I'm stuck in this hole, he told himself. I wish they'd pulled the damned clearance!

He sighed. There was nothing he could do about any of that now. He'd just have to live through his time in purgatory and hope that the Corps would find a nice little war somewhere so he could get back into the action—where he belonged!

In the meantime, he just had to keep a bored eye on the damned Depot.

"Company, Gunny," his assistant sang out from the office. "Looks like a deuce-and-a-half. From Headquarters maybe."

It was, indeed, a two and a half-ton truck—but the markings on its bumpers didn't match any unit from inside the Depot.

"What can I do for you?" Crews asked the Corporal that stepped out of the cab.

"I have requisitions for three containers of your munitions," the very young-looking man told him, pulling a set of flimsy papers from his pocket. "I'd like to get them ASAP," he looked up. "Before it starts to rain."

"It doesn't rain at Quantico," Crews told him. "God just pees on us occasionally." He looked through the papers. "These seem to be in order but I'm going to have to verify them."

"Of course. Go right ahead," the youngish corporal leaned back against the bumper of his truck. "I'll wait."

Crews brought up the proper address on his office computer and entered the routing number and clearance codes from the requisition form, then entered his own ID code and requested verification.

It came back almost instantaneously.

"Okay," Crews stepped back outside. "Come on—let's get you loaded up so you can go back to wherever it is you're going."

"I'm ordered to drop these in the District," the Corporal grinned. "Somebody wants them for a display there."

"A display?" Crews shook his head as he helped load the first of the SA containers onto a hand truck. "There's enough blood agent in each of these things to kill a thousand people!"

"My boss figured more like five thousand," the Corporal smiled. "So I'll be sure to handle them very carefully!"

Five minutes later, the deuce and a half was gone, as were three containers of blood agent

And what was left of Gunnery Sergeant Crews' career.

**

ARLINGTON NATIONAL CEMETARY— ARLINGTON VA.

"I thought I might find you here," Farrell had gone to the motel room the agency booked for Sean, planning on taking the youngster to breakfast. When he found the room empty, he thought the youngster might have given in to despair and gone home.

Then he realized the truth.

"Talking to your dad?" He glanced at the marble marker that indicated the elder Piper's final resting spot.

"Yeah." Sean was standing in front of the gravesite, staring at the marker. "I've been wondering what he would do if he was in my shoes."

"What do you mean?"

"Dad died trying to save other lives—you've told me that he might have been able to get away but didn't even try." Sean looked at the older man. "Can I do less?"

"Listen..."

"No," Sean shook his head. "If I allow them to take me, they'll stop trying to crash airplanes." His face clouded. "I had a look at what's left of Union Station this morning. I saw crews carrying out body bag after body bag..."

"Sean, we can't just give Ramnarain and the others what they want. If we do," Farrell spread his hands. "They'll just come back for more—again and again." He looked at his young friend. "The only way to stop people like them is the way your father did." His face went hard. "We have to find and kill them like the animals they are."

"Has anyone had any luck finding them?"

"Not yet. We're sure they're in one of the other shelters, but..."

"But what?"

"We're having trouble figuring out where those shelters are." Farrell shrugged. "Most of them were closed down in the seventies and it appears that all of the records have been lost..."

"Or destroyed."

"Or that." Farrell nodded. "The FBI is looking for some of the officials who approved the placement of the shelters." He grinned. "One or two of them may still be alive but I'd be surprised if they remember anything about the project..."

"So if we can't find them, what can we do?"

"We try something else!" Farrell's voice was harsh. "We do not pay them—we never pay terrorists—and we damned sure do not give up one of our own!"

"If there's no other way ..."

"Sean, trust me." Farrell held out a hand. "Mary Max would never approve such a thing."

"What about her boss? Or his?" Sean shook his head. "It might be better if..."

There was a humming whine in the distance.

"What's that?" Sean looked around.

"Nothing." Farrell shook his head. "The groundskeepers are mowing the grass—they have to do it pretty much every day this time of year..." Farrell slapped himself on the forehead. "Of course!"

"What?"

"Why does the grass grow so quickly?"

"I don't know," Sean looked around. "They water it?"

"Water!" Farrell nodded slowly. "Those bunkers have to be getting water from somewhere!"

"They could have their own wells..."

"They could," Farrell's face fell. "Yeah, they could..."

"Power!" Sean's eyes lit up. "They'll have to have a source of power! Even if they have their own wells, they'll need pumps!"

"Let's get back to the office." Farrell made a quick gesture. "We'll get the FBI working on this."

"Why them and not us?"

166

"They have the manpower to do it quickly—and time is important."

"Okay," Sean's eyes darkened as he thought about what would happen if they didn't find Ramnarain soon. "Quicker is better."

"If the FBI can find a spot in Northern Virginia that's suddenly drawing water and/or power…"

"We'll know where Ramnarain and the others have set up their new headquarters." Sean followed him as he headed for the car. "And once we know where they are…"

"We'll know just what to do next!"

"I just hope we find them in time," Sean looked at his watch. "We have less than fifteen hours left."

"There's something else we can do," Farrell looked at his young charge. "If you're up for it…"

***

INTERSTATE 95-NORTH OF QUANTICO VA.
NOON

"I got what you wanted," Mike reported over his cell phone once he was back on the highway. "Those requisition papers worked just as well as you said they would."

"The papers," Ramnarain told him. "And our hack into their verification system." The older man chuckled. "It was almost too easy!"

"Do you want me to take the stuff straight to your location?"

"As quickly as you can. I'd like to have your truck and its cargo back under cover before anyone realizes what happened."

"Yes sir," Mike answered. "You know, I kinda like the way this uniform makes me look ..."

"You'd never make it in the military," Ramnarain chuckled. "And Carole would kill you if you tried to join!"

"Yeah," Mike nodded. "I guess you're right."

"Watch your speed; don't bump your cargo around too much..."

"Don't worry," Mike smiled as a Highway Patrol car passed by, speeding in the other direction. "I won't take any chances."

***

UNION STATION—WASHINGTON D.C.

"How much time do we have left?" Sean was carefully studying the screen of the brand-new laptop Farrell had requisitioned from the FBI.

"Two hours," Farrell replied. "But there shouldn't be anything in the air at this point—the FAA pancaked everything six hours ago."

The two men were standing in the center of what had once been the heart of Union Station. The last smoldering fires were out and most of the bodies had been located and removed although it would take a few days for the NTSB to recover what was left of the aircraft, Farrell had decided to make use of that time to see if Sean's theory of what had happened could be proven.

"Just what are we looking for?" The ex-CIA man asked. "I mean, you thought there was a device somewhere in the plane to pick up signals—not send them."

"That's partially correct," Sean frowned as he worked his keyboard. "I'm sending out a typical Bluetooth signal right now—the kind that generates a handshake to, for example, connect a phone with an earbud..." He showed Farrell the visual representation of the signal on his screen. "If they did use that kind of receiver to hack into the plane's navigation systems, it has to talk to those systems using this kind of technology. It follows that if I send out a signal, it should pick it up and respond in some fashion..."

"I thought airline systems of that kind were impenetrable..."

"They're supposed to be." Sean looked at his screen, frowned and changed the signal strength. "But they're not. The avionics package reports location and speed to the aircraft's entertainment system." He leaned closer to his screen. "That's what allows those little progress maps on the TV screens to work.

He looked at Farrell. "And the engines send info—including data from the avionics package--to the Aircraft manufacturer." He gestured. "You remember how big a flap that information caused when that Malaysian flight disappeared a year or so ago."

"Boeing said they were getting engine signals long after the plane was supposed to have gone into the sea," Farrell nodded, recalling the incident.

"The EICAS—that's the Engine-Indicating and Crew-Alerting System—gets its data from a hydro mechanical controller with an electronic interface, called the an EEC. If you can override the EEC, you can take control of both the engines and the operating systems."

"But how?"

"The only way I can see that might work is by connecting a Bluetooth device directly to the EEC." Sean shrugged. "I'm not sure how you would do that but…" He stopped in front of a pile of rubble near what had been a restaurant. "Look here!"

"What is it?" Farrell asked, staring at a mass of burned circuitry.

"That, I believe," Sean pointed to a reddish-black bit of plastic still partially plugged into a circuit panel. "Is the Bluetooth device I've been looking for." He looked at his partner. "Would it be alright to touch it?"

"The NTSB will want to be here when you do," Farrell pulled out his phone and punched in a number. "Take some pictures so we have a record of where it was found."

"Already on that," Sean had also been supplied with a brand-new FBI cellphone which he now used to get hi-definition photos of the suspect board. "How long before we can examine it?"

Farrell held up a finger as he spoke to someone on his own phone, then nodded and hung up. "They'll be here in ten minutes." He punched in a second number. "I'm going to get the FBI out here too—their CSU guys might be able to get some kind of physical evidence off that thing."

"Why bother?" Sean stepped back, looking at the ruined building lying all around him. "We know who's behind it."

"We may have to prove they did it in a court of law." Farrell shrugged. "It's a pain but it is part of the job."

"What's going on with the ransom?"

"Mary Max will try to 'negotiate' with Ramnarain."

"Why?"

"To give us time to find him," Farrell gestured to the burned out circuit board. "Or figure out how he's doing it so we can stop him from doing it again."

Sean stared at the lump of plastic, hoping against hope that it would lead him to Ramnarain...

And Halle, he told himself. I owe her an apology...

***

UNKNOWN LOCATION #2-
NORTHEASTERN VIRGINIA

"Okay, just what are you two thinking?" Carole, supported by Mike, who was, for some reason, still wearing his Marine uniform, asked as she confronted Ramnarain and Halle in one of the offices. "Why in hell would you ask the Feds to give us money but add the Piper kid to the price?

"He's mine!" Halle's eyes burned with the intensity of her hatred. "I need to get my revenge on him!"

"Dream on," Carole snarled. "They won't just 'give' us an innocent civilian—it would destroy them politically! The cries for Impeachment would be loud enough for us to hear them down here!"

171

"How many planes can they lose," Ramnarain put in. "Before they get the same cries?"

"That's different," She shook her head. "You know it and the people we're dealing with know it!"

"There are other things we can do—things that will cause a lot more casualties for your 'people' to worry about!'"

"You're talking about the SA Mike brought in?" Carole snarled. "You think killing more people will convince them to give us the kid?" She shook her head. "It'll just make them that much more determined to find and kill us!"

"They'll never..."

"Bullshit!" Carole glared at Ramnarain. "Some of the CIA and FBI guys are smart! They'll figure out a way to find us and when they do..."

"They'll also find the SA," Ms. Waterson put in as she entered the room. "I suspect that will give them a bit of a surprise."

"You're planning on setting a trap?" Carole's eyes narrowed. "How is that going to get us the ransom money?"

"There's more at stake here than a few million dollars of ransom money," Ramnarain told the girl. "Far more."

"Not for me." Carole's snarl matched his. "I signed up for the money— nothing else."

"Well," Ramnarain smiled. "The situation has changed—and you have no choice but to change right along with it," he raised an eyebrow. "I hope that's understood?"

Carole caught a movement out of the corner of her eye and saw that Ms. Waterson hadn't come in alone—she had brought three burly guards, each of them brandishing an automatic weapon.

"I see," Carole took a deep breath and looked at Ramnarain. "This was the plan all the time, wasn't it?"

He shrugged.

"What do I get out of it?"

"Just what I promised," he looked at her, a smile on his face. "More money than you can possibly spend," he raised his hands, palms up. "And, assuming you don't do anything stupid, a nice long life in which to spend it." He chuckled. "That is what you are after," he smiled into Carole's unhappy face. "Is it not?"

When Carole said nothing, Ramnarain turned away and headed for his office. Ms. Waterson, Halle, and the guards a step or two behind him.

Carole watched them go, knowing that the game had changed and wondering if she still wanted to play…

CHAPTER TWENTY-TWO

J. EDGAR HOOVER BUILDING
WASHINGTON D.C.

"This is a very interesting piece of tech," the FBI electronics expert shook his head admiringly as he held the tiny square of plastic up in front of him. "At first glance it appears to be just another cheap computer chip—the kind you can purchase on any number of internet sites, but if you go deeper...

The expert looked at Mary Max. "There's a lot more to it." He held up the chip. "This single chip is capable, once activated, of taking control of the EEC—the Electronic Engine Controls—used by nearly all aircraft built by either Boeing or Airbus." He shook his head as he stared at the chip. "It's a brilliant piece of work."

"How do outsiders use the chip to gain control of the EEC?" The FBI agent-in-charge asked.

"The chip has a Bluetooth built in. To use it, you would first have to access the aircraft's Wi-Fi system."

"Which you can do through the entertainment system," Sean interjected.

"Precisely." The electronics man nodded. "Once you do that, you have full access—and complete control over the aircraft." He looked around the table. "You can do pretty much anything you want at that point."

"What if the pilot turned the entertainment systems off?"

"It wouldn't do any good once control was established," the expert shrugged. "There's a hardwired command sequence built into this thing that takes control of the entertainment and Wi-Fi systems as soon as it's activated. After that, the pilot has no more chance to turn it off than he has of controlling the aircraft once the EEC is overridden."

"Do we know where this was made?" Ms. Dizon asked.

"Not in the US," the expert told her. "Beyond that, I couldn't say without more time to study it."

"Thank you." Mary Max looked around the now crowded room. "We will assume for the moment that Dr. Ramnarain designed this chip— and that he had confederates outside the country manufacture it for him." She looked around. "The real question is—how did he get it into the planes?"

"Most aircraft in this country," the FAA representative said. "Have full maintenance checks at regular intervals." He nodded at the chip. "It would probably have been possible to insert this during one of those checks."

"That argues that he has even more confederates!" Ms. Dizon said. "Confederates who work for the airlines."

"Not necessarily," the FAA man put in. "New components are added all the time—all it would take was paperwork from the manufacturer instructing the maintenance crews to install the chip."

"And Ramnarain's people have already shown us they can handle phony paperwork with no trouble," Farrell pointed out.

The FAA man nodded. "We'll have to go over the records of every plane with an EEC and Entertainment system. Hopefully we'll find the paperwork."

"While you're doing that, we'll have to have every other plane with this kind of system checked for such a chip," Mary Max' voice was tired—she hadn't had much sleep since Farrell first called her two—or was it three—days ago. "That check will have to be overseen by people we can completely trust."

"The FAA doesn't have the resources to take on that kind of volume."

"The military does," Ms. Dizon put in. "Tell me how many people you'll need and I will get with the necessary commanders and see that they're made available."

"It's just a stopgap unless we find Ramnarain and his merry band," Farrell told them. "Eventually they'll come up with something else to use." He looked around the table. "They might already have something in place!"

"About that," Mary Max turned to the FBI representative. "Have you had any luck finding more of those bunkers?"

He shook his head.

"Have you checked infrared sources?" Sean asked, looking at Farrell as he did so. "We know they have to have a power source—they need heat and an air exchanger if they're underground—that should show up on IR."

"It's an idea," the FBI man made a note. "I'll see if we can get a couple of choppers for a search..."

"The Marines will give you what you need," Ms. Dizon was already punching an order into her phone. "I'll have them ready in less than an hour!"

***

UNKNOWN LOCATION #2- NORTHEASTERN VIRGINIA

"Come on!" Carole led Mike down the corridor that, she knew, led to the generator room and an unguarded access point. "We've got to get out of here before they notice we're missing!"

"Why?" Mike was dragging his heels a bit. "I mean, we've always trusted Dr. Ramnarain."

"That was when he was making sense." She looked into his face. "Do you really think that storing three canisters of blood agent over our heads makes sense?"

"He says he has a plan to use it…"

"He said he had a plan for getting us fifty million in protection money," she led him around a tight corner. "Do we have our share yet?"

"That's because Halle needs to get her hands on Sean Piper…"

"Why is that our problem?" Carole led them to a door inset into the concrete of the lower corridor. "We joined up so we could make the money we need to live our lives in comfort. We did not agree to put that off while we help a crazy bitch get revenge on the guy who offed her boyfriend!"

"Yeah, but…"

"No buts!" Carole pushed the door open, revealing a seemingly never-ending vista of pine trees. "We've got to get away from this place!"

"No!" Mike dug in his heels. "I trust the professor." He crossed his arms, staring at her. "I'm not going!"

"But Mike…"

"You said it yourself," he held his hands out. "No buts."

"Mike," she threw her arms around him. "Honey…"

"Carole, I love you dearly," he pushed her shoulders away. "But I am not ready to quit on the professor! If you are…" He looked into her eyes and blinked when he saw the tears there. "Well," he choked back a sob. "I wish you good luck."

They stood there for a long moment, than Carole took a deep breath. "All right," she hugged him tight. "We'll stay," she shook her head. "But if you're wrong…"

"I'm not wrong." He held her to him. "The Professor knows what he's doing. This will all turn out just fine."

"I'm glad you think so." Ramnarain said from somewhere behind them. "Now, I would appreciate it if you would get ready to move."

"Move?" Carole looked at him. "We just got here!"

"We did, but I don't think this location is secure anymore," he pointed outside where the open door was throwing a long trail of yellow light across the black brush.

"Shit!"

CHAPTER TWENTY-THREE

"Sean!" Farrell pounded on the door to his partner's room. "Wake up Sean!"

"What?" The youngster staggered to the door and opened it. "What time is it?"

"Doesn't matter." Farrell brushed past him. "We found something."

"What?"

"Look!" Farrell handed the youngster a tablet on which a light could be seen in the middle of a forest. "That was taken by one of our keyhole satellites about two hours ago." He shook his head. "It took a while for the operator to realize what he was seeing."

"I don't blame him for not figuring it out more quickly." Sean stared at the image. "Where is this?"

"That's a section of the Monongahela National Forest—there should be nothing there with any lights."

"It's another bunker!"

"Must be." He gestured. "There's a chopper with a SWAT team waiting for us—get your clothes on!"

***

Fifteen minutes later, the two were airborne, sharing the personnel bay of a Blackhawk with a four-man FBI team.

"Remember," Farrell told them over the headset intercoms. "Do not—I repeat, DO NOT enter without my approval."

179

"Yes sir," the senior agent—the same one who had been with them when they last entered a bunker—replied. "Our orders are to do whatever you say."

"Good." Farrell looked over the forest below. "We're almost there—if we can't find an LZ, we're going to have to go down with a penetrator."

"My men are trained for that, sir."

"Sean," Farrell looked at his partner. "Think you can do it?"

"I've done it a dozen times before," the youngster smiled. "But only in video games."

"There's nothing to it," the FBI man nearest him slapped him on the back. "Just hold on tight and we'll get you down!"

Sean nodded—but couldn't help but feel relieved when they discovered a large open meadow less than a hundred yards south of the bunker's position.

Farrell, Sean, and the team began final preparations for their assault as the chopper approached the landing zone...

"Commo check—turn your radios on!" Farrell took off his intercom helmet and inserted an earbud pre-tuned to the radio clipped to his belt. He motioned for the others to do the same and, when he was sure they were all ready, held up two fingers.

"Channel 2."

Everyone nodded and adjusted their gear, then:

"Everyone hear me?" Farrell asked.

"Got you five by," the FBI leader told him.

"Me too," Sean added.

"Okay," Farrell put his right foot on the skid and took a grip on the door frame with his left hand. "Get ready..."

The chopper steadied when it was about five feet from the ground at which point Farrell dropped off the skid.

"Everyone out!" Came over the earbuds!

Sean was already on the ground, a step behind his partner, his Glock held a bit too tightly in a sweaty hand.

"There's a good spot over there!" Farrell pointed at a copse of trees just in front of a now clearly visible bunker door. "Get over there and give the rest of us cover!"

Sean nodded and sprinted for the indicated position. He was almost there when the first shots were fired...

***

Crap! Sean dove for cover as bullets whizzed through the trees around him. What do I do now?

He took a quick look back at the chopper, hoping that Farrell and the FBI team were running up to support him.

They weren't, they were too busy diving for cover as the chopper lifted off.

I have to do something, he told himself. I can't just sit here and let them get shot!

He ducked as more bullets came his way.

What would Dad do?

Even as the question crossed his mind, the world changed around him. Everything slowed down—like a film running in slow motion. His vision changed until everything around him was crystal clear...

I'm not scared anymore! Sean realized as he rolled into more secure cover and raised his weapon. It's like… He frowned. It's like Dad's here with me!

That's Impossible, of course. He smiled. But it's nice to have that feeling!

Sean flicked the safety of his Glock to 'OFF' and settled into position. The best way to get them to stop shooting at me and the others, he told himself. Is to take the fight to them!

He took a deep breath, and took a second to relax and get his breathing under control—just as he had been taught.

Then, calm once again, he laid the Glock over his left elbow to give himself a makeshift firing rest and searched the opening for the source of the fire.

Let's see what we can see … He centered the Glock's iron sights at the midpoint of the bunker entrance and waited for someone to move. Almost immediately, he saw a muzzle flash at one side of the opening, bright enough in the pre-dawn darkness to limn the man firing in light.

There's one! Sean shifted his aim just a bit and centered his sights on the spot he had noted--just to his left and slightly above the muzzle flash.

He squeezed the Glock's trigger…

***

I should have let the kid take a rifle, Farrell thought as he watched Sean fire toward the unseen shooters inside the mouth of the bunker. He'd have been more useful giving us cover…

There was a cry from the bunker and the clatter of a rifle falling to the ground.

Maybe I should stop worrying about him... Farrell saw Sean calmly search for another target. And start worrying about the rest of us!

Over the next few moments, the youngster fired three more times—each shot was followed by the clatter of a body falling to the floor of the bunker entrance.

Then it got very quiet...

"Cover me," Farrell muttered into his earbud as he scrambled across the open area and slid into cover directly across from Sean who was slipping a fresh magazine into his weapon.

There was no response from the bunker.

"Think you got them all?" He asked Sean.

"Nothing's moving in there, anymore." The youngster answered, his eyes never leaving the target area. "Only one way to find out if anyone's still alive."

He rose to his feet and sprinted toward the pre-fab hut that guarded the entrance to the bunker, slamming into the wall on one side and immediately flattening himself with his weapon pointed toward the open door.

"Damn it, Sean!" Farrell hissed even as he followed the boy's example and slammed into position on the opposite side. "You should have let the FBI guys do that!"

"They're so far behind us that they could run into an ambush on the way here!" Sean grinned at his partner. "Besides, it felt right to do it this way."

"Your father always took the lead," Farrell shook his head. "You're a lot like him--in too many ways!" He swung into the doorway, handgun searching for a target. "Let's see what they were so intent on protecting!"

***

It took the FBI team a few minutes to catch up. By that time, Sean and Farrell had checked the men who had been left to guard the entrance.

All were dead.

"I recognize two of them from my time in the compound," Sean nodded at the bodies. "The others are new to me."

"Pretty good shooting," Farrell told him. "They're all wearing body armor and yet you dropped each with a single shot."

"Body armor doesn't protect the head," the youngster shrugged. "If one of them had been taller, I might have missed."

"I doubt that," Farrell waved for the FBI leader to join them. "We've got to get all the way inside," he looked at the SWAT team members. "Break down the door and get inside—we'll follow."

"Yes sir," the agent motioned to his men.

"Sean," Farrell turned to his partner. "If you haven't already done so, you should reload."

"Way ahead of you on that."

"Good." Farrell smiled back. "I hope you kept the other magazine."

"Of course," Sean's smile widened. "I might need those extra rounds later."

"Wise ass!"

"Hey," Sean shrugged. "Dad always said that you should change a depleted magazine when you have the opportunity—but that you should always keep the partially-used mag in case you need it later."

"That's good advice." Farrell told him. "Your father knew what he was doing when he trained you."

"Thanks." Sean looked toward the door. "Can we see what's inside now?"

At Farrell's gesture, the FBI team stepped forward, two of them were carrying a ram they'd brought to knock down the inside door.

"Try the doorknob first," Sean told them. "It might not be locked."

They tried—and it was locked--but not securely enough to hold up against the FBI ram.

"Okay," Farrell took a quick peek through the smashed-open door. "I want two of the armored SWAT team members in front. Sean and I will stay in the middle and the rest of you," he pointed at the agent-in-charge. "Watch our six."

"Roger," the FBI man indicated which of his men would take point. "No shooting unless they shoot at you." He told them. "We want prisoners—not corpses."

The two men nodded and stepped through the door, rifles questing into the darkness of a corridor that led sharply left.

"Let's go," Farrell moved in behind them, his pistol up and ready for anything. Sean stayed just behind him and to the right, covering his partner's blind side.

They started down the long corridor, moving very carefully...

***

"Don't shoot!" Carole stood in the middle of the room, hands over her head. "Please!"

185

"Carole?" Sean walked toward her while Farrell angled away so it would be the girl caught in the crossfire if things went wrong. "Where's Ramnarain?"

"Gone!" She shook her head. "He left a couple of hours ago—after locking us into this place."

"Us?"

"Donna's back there," Carole gestured vaguely. "So is Bob…"

"Where're Mike and Halle?"

"Halle left with Ramnarain," Carole looked into Sean's eyes. "She really hates you!"

"And Mike?"

"He's on the couch." Carole shivered. "Ramnarain tested the SA on him…"

"SA!" Farrell head jerked toward the girl. "That's a blood agent!"

"Yeah," Carole nodded. "I know."

"Okay," Sean kept his voice level, friendly. "Show us where Mike is."

A moment later they were looking down on the body of Michael Mize. His face was blue-gray in color and contorted from his final spasms.

"He couldn't breathe," Carole told them. "Just couldn't…"

"We've got to get a CBR team here soonest," Farrell grabbed for his phone. "And find the SA before Ramnarain can release it…"

"He's got a plan," Carole told them. "The 'HEMO' plan." She chuckled. "He told us we were gonna be rich!" Her laugh grew louder and wilder as she slumped to the floor, reaching out to touch her dead partner's hands. "Rich enough to live our lives together in comfort!" She continued to laugh until tears filled her eyes and she collapsed in a heap, quietly sobbing…

CHAPTER TWENTY-FOUR

J. EDGAR HOOVER BUILDING,
WASHINGTON DC

"It appears that someone." Security camera footage of Mike in the military-marked deuce and a half appeared on the big screen. "Signed out three canisters of SA from the Marine Depot in Quantico,"

Mary Max's briefing now included more than thirty people, all of them seated in one of the two large lecture halls on the ground floor of FBI headquarters.

"Examination of the documents tells us they are near-perfect forgeries."

"Isn't there a verification system?" Colonel Granville asked. "I thought we set that up at all stateside installations."

"There is such a system—but it was hacked to allow the requisition to go through."

"Didn't the Sergeant of the Guard realize that the kid driving the truck was obviously not a Marine?" Granville was the newly-appointed military attaché to the group. "I mean, look at him!"

"Gunnery Sergeant Crews has been relieved of duty and will be questioned." Mary Max shook her head. "I believe that we will find that he was just lazy and bored." She looked at the group. "As for the stolen material—we now know that it was SA in Gaseous form—a weaponized-version of 'Cyanogen chloride/hydrogen cyanide'." She glanced at her notes. "Apparently that is an agent that prevents cells from using oxygen in the blood." She looked around the room. "The cells then go into anaerobic respiration which creates an excess of lactic acid which causes metabolic acidosis and leads to seizures and death." She shook her head. "It's nasty stuff."

"I thought we destroyed our chemical arsenal." Ms. Dizon asked.

"We did." Mary Max looked at the Presidential Aide. "But some samples were kept in case of need." She looked at the image of Sgt. Crews on the big TV. "Under heavy guard."

"How deadly is it?" The FBI Agent-in-Chief asked.

"Very," Mary Max told him. "It works quickly and in only requires a very small concentration in the body to be fatal."

"Great," the FBI man looked around the table and swallowed before continuing. "I think we may now know why this is happening."

Mary Max looked at him. "Yes…"

"We've done an updated background check on Professor Ramnarain." The Agent rubbed his chin. "It appears that he had a son…

"Had?"

"The younger Ramnarain was an archaeologist, the agent sighed. "He was visiting a dig near Kabul, Afghanistan." The agent looked around the room. "An American drone fired a missile into the compound, destroying it and killing all the workers there." He looked at the others. "The operator mixed up his co-ordinates…"

"Great," Farrell muttered. "That explains a lot."

"There's more." The agent looked at Mary Max. "We finally found some information on Ms. Waterson. It seems that she too lost someone to one of our drone strikes," he looked at the others. "In her case, it was a husband and two children."

"How…"

"Ms. Waterson was one of ours…" The CIA representative spoke up. "She married an Iranian while working in Syria. They couldn't live in Iran so they stayed where they were. He was a historian working on a book about the Roman ruins in Palmyra…"

"What happened?" Mary Max asked.

"He got involved with the Free Syrian Army. He was in Homs when one of our Reapers hit the wrong target…"

"Great." Farrell shook his head. "Both of them want American blood." He looked at the CIA agent. "Anything else? Do you have something that might help us find these people?"

The man shook his head.

"Okay," Mary Max stood up. "It's clear that Professor Ramnarain is planning something big— something that involves the use of the SA…" She glanced at Farrell. "We did hope that we could get an insight into his plans when we captured the computers in the second bunker…"

"They were all wiped," he reported. "And the hard disks were smashed." He shook his head. "There was nothing left to be found."

"Our…" Mary Max sucked her lip. "Our prisoners have no idea what his plan entails?"

"Ms. Ross told us that the only one who might know the whole story is Halle—and she left with

Ramnarain and Waterson. The others were never briefed on HEMO."

"I see…"

"We might be able to get something from one of the computer mother boards." Sean put in. "It won't be much, but there might be something in the cache."

"Is that being checked?"

"As we speak," the FBI Agent-in-Charge nodded. "We have some of our top people working on it."

"All right," Mary Max looked around the table. "We have roadblocks on all major roads and guards at every train and bus station. We should be able to pick Ramnarain up before he can put his plan into effect…"

"No." Farrell shook his head. "We're looking at this wrong." He looked at Mary Max. "The plane crashes have to be part of his master plan—they don't make sense otherwise."

"He asked for money…"

"Not in a serious way," Farrell bit his lower lip. "Just seriously enough to keep the kids happy so they'd continue to do his bidding." He shook his head. "I think the crashes were just to throw us off balance and maybe…"

He looked at Mary Max as a thought struck him. "What's the airline situation right now?"

"Everything is grounded until each plane is checked for those chips you and Sean discovered."

"And when that happens?"

"The sky is going to get pretty crowded until the airlines finally get all their passengers sorted out."

"What's flying in the meantime?"

"Just military stuff." She frowned as she looked at her list. "Cargo jets—none of the military planes have entertainment systems… Helicopters, fighters on patrol…"

"He's going to use military lift to carry the SA!"

"How?"

"I don't know but it's the only thing that makes sense." Farrell glanced at the others around the table. "You saw how easy it was for him to fake the paperwork he needed to acquire the SA," His eyes locked on the Military advisor. "He could get a plane or a helicopter the same way."

Mary Max nodded. "That makes sense." She came to a quick decision. "Follow up on that." She looked at Farrell. "See if you and your partner can come up with some information we can act on." She turned to the FBI representative. "In the meantime, I want the Bureau to work on getting us full psych profiles on Ramnarain and Waterson. Maybe that will give us something."

"Yes Ma'am," the Agent-in-Charge nodded.

"The rest of you," Mary Max made a sweeping gesture. "Go over the intelligence we've assembled, see if anyone can come up with any way to find Ramnarain's new hide-out—-and for God's Sake, make sure he doesn't 'requisition' anything else!"

She didn't know it, but it was too late for that last order to matter...

CHAPTER TWENTY-FIVE

ARMY HELICOPTER DEPOT--FORT RUCKER, ALABAMA

"This all seems to be in order," Captain Jay Fielding said as he scanned the documents that had been presented to his clerk. "I will, of course, have to verify."

"Of course," Halle smiled at him, giving him enough voltage to ensure he was paying more attention to her than he was to his computer. "Please do."

Fielding punched in the most recent address he had for the process—and was rewarded with a proper verification code.

"All right, Warrant Officer…"

"Piper," Halle gave him another smile. "How soon can you have the bird ready?"

"We have one of the flight line right now," the Captain smiled at her. "It's fully fueled and ready to go."

"Good," Halle nodded. "I'll get my gear loaded." She offered the Captain her hand. "It's been a pleasure dealing with you, sir."

"And with you, Ms. Piper." The officer's smile widened. "Be sure to give my regards to the Colonel."

"I most certainly will." Halle raised the voltage on her smile a notch. "And I promise to get the chopper back to you just as soon as we're done with it!"

"That'll be fine." He gave her a sketchy salute. "I'll look forward to seeing you then." He watched as she returned his salute and turned toward the door. Nice-looking woman, he thought as she swayed her way out. I wonder how she got into the Army?

He shrugged and returned to his paperwork. It really doesn't matter. He glanced at the door, hoping for one more look. She's working for the brass—they're never going to pass her along to someone like me.

He was fantasizing the kinds of things he could do if that particular girl ever did come under his command when he heard the motor of the Sikorsky UH-60 Black Hawk start up…

Ah well, he thought. So much for that fantasy!

***

J. EDGAR HOOVER BUILDING, WASHINGTON DC

"Got something," Mary Max stepped into Farrell's office, brandishing a tablet. "Look!"

Sean moved to Farrell's side and together, they watched the surveillance video.

"That's Halle!" Sean said as a young woman in uniform presented her credentials to a gate guard. "Where is this?"

"Fort Rucker, Alabama," Mary Max told him. "Keep watching, there's more."

Sean and Farrell watched intently as the image switched to a second camera, this one overlooking a flight line of Blackhawk helicopters. Halfway down that line, Halle was climbing into one of the

194

choppers and signaling the ground crew to pull the chocks.

"Can she fly that thing?" Farrell asked.

"Anyone who's willing to put in the time on a PS-2 can learn to fly a Blackhawk," Sean answered. "It's finding a way to get into a real pilot seat that's difficult."

"Not for these people, apparently." Mary Max shook her head sadly. "This girl..." She nodded at the screen where Halle and the Blackhawk were lifting from the ground. "Had a perfectly authentic-looking set of orders to transfer a helicopter from the base in Alabama to the command of a Colonel in North Carolina." She looked at the two men. "It was verified via computer and the commander just waved 'Warrant Officer Piper'," she looked at Sean. "Into the blue."

"Piper?"

"Yeah," Mary Max nodded. "She used your name on her credentials."

"They can use the Blackhawk to fly the SA over any target they choose," Farrell stated. "It's heavier than air so all they'd have to do is pour it out the door and let the slipstream carry it away from them."

"How much range does one of those things have?" Sean asked. "Because as far as we know, the SA is still somewhere in Virginia."

"Around three-hundred fifty miles."

"And how far away is Fort Rucker?"

"I don't know—eight hundred miles?"

"They'd have to refuel at least once," Sean nodded. "If we could figure out where..."

"Unless I'm mistaken," Farrell turned to his desktop computer. "Army Blackhawk's have a GPS positioning system..." He typed in a series of commands. "We'll need more information on this particular chopper to zero in on it."

"You'll get it," Mary Max told him. "Do you think the target is going to be Washington?"

"I can't see any other possibilities," Farrell told her. "Both Ramnarain and Waterson have a grudge against the people here so where else would they hit?"

"I'll have to get interceptors into the air..."

"You can't," Farrell shook his head. "If you shoot the thing down, you'll spread the SA over an even wider area." He looked at Sean. "We either have to take it—and the blood agent containers—intact or put in in the water somewhere."

"Let's get the GPS data," Sean told him. "We can track the chopper and figure out where he's going to land to refuel."

"We'll have to be in the air ourselves if we're going to have any chance to intercept them..."

"I'll get choppers for you and your FBI team—along with all the other information you might need."

"Make it fast, Mary Max." Farrell told her. "A Blackhawk can do a hundred and eighty miles an hour—that puts it just about five hours away."

"Five hours." She nodded. "I'll pass that up the line as well. You two get whatever you think you'll need—I'll have a chopper ready to go in ten minutes."

"Where?"

"Out there!" She pointed to the National Mall. "I'll have them put it down on the lawn."

"Roger that," Farrell nodded. "We'll be ready."

CHAPTER TWENTY-SIX

"Bastard kept looking at my ass!" Halle muttered to no one in particular. "Like only my looks mean anything!"

"It doesn't matter, my dear." Ms. Waterson told her. "You got the helicopter and nobody is the wiser."

"For now," Ramnarain grunted as he shifted the position of one of the canisters of SA in the passenger compartment. "They'll figure it out quickly enough."

"How long to get to our target?" Waterson asked.

"Maybe six hours," Halle answered. "Depends on where we set down to refuel."

"We don't have the range to go all the way?"

"This is a helicopter!" Halle shook her head. "It's not designed for long-range travel."

"There's a helicopter charter company just south of Petersburg, Virginia—near the North Carolina border." Ramnarain told her. "It has all the fuel we'll need on hand."

"Good." Halle nodded. "Find it on the map and show me."

"It's right here," Ramnarain pulled out the aviation map in question and held it up for Halle to take a look. "I'll set the co-ordinates into the GPS system."

Halle glanced at the gauges, then at the display for the new destination. "We'll be there in just under five hours." She looked at the other two.

"Make sure we have any paperwork we might need."

"I already printed it out."

"Good," Halle yawned. "You know, it's boring up here without a lot of other air traffic."

"It's better this way," Ms. Waterson told her. "With non-military traffic grounded, we don't have to deal with multiple control towers—we just ignore any calls and by the time they sort things out…" She smiled a hard smile. "It'll all be over."

"I wish I could take care of Sean Piper before we leave the country!"

"Too dangerous," Ramnarain shook his head. "Wait until things cool down a little—then either hire someone to take him out or find a way to do it yourself." He smiled. "Things will, after all, be somewhat chaotic here for the next year or two."

"Besides," Ms. Waterson put in. "It's quite possible that we'll kill him with the SA. He was in Washington the last time we heard from him."

"I hope he's not there. I hope he's safe!" Halle shook her head. "I want to look right into his eyes when I kill him." She sighed. "The way he looked into Jayson's…"

She shook the overwhelming emotion away before it could consume her and turned her attention back to the helicopter…

***

THE NATIONAL MALL, WASHINGTON D.C.

"Judging by the GPS settings, Ramnarain's chopper is heading for a small helipad near Petersburg—probably to refuel." Sean told the pilot as, ignoring the eyes of the tourists watching from behind cordons set up by Capital police, he climbed into the Blackhawk. "I've done some calculations and if you really redline this thing, we should be able to get there first."

"We'll do our best," the pilot nodded and set the destination information into his own navigational system. "Will the local police be on hand?"

"God, I hope not!" Farrell shook his head. "We've alerted them, of course, but we've asked that they just cordon off the area—keep it clear of civilians. There's no telling what would happen if some half-trained redneck cop opened fire on a helicopter full of SA!"

"It's all up to us, then?"

"You got it." Farrell gestured for the FBI team to strap in. "Now get this thing into the air! Time's-a-wastin'!"

The pilot nodded and settled back into his seat, feeding power to the overhead rotors that smoothly lifted the Blackhawk from the green grass of the National Mall...

CHAPTER TWENTY-SEVEN

"We've got to speed up or we're not going to make it there before they arrive," Sean reported from his position in the back of the chopper. He was using his laptop to monitor the position of Halle's Blackhawk and it was telling him that she was just a few miles short of the North Carolina border.

"We still have time to make it," Farrell nudged the pilot. "Drop the nose and let's move!"

"But look at the engine revs! If it overheats…"

"We'll buy you another one!" Farrell glared at him. "Now get this piece of crap moving!"

Reluctantly, the pilot ran the throttle up to full and dropped the nose, the chopper sped up to just over one-eighty.

"That's better," Sean said from the back seat. "Don't let up!"

The FBI Blackhawk hurtled across the Richmond metropolitan area at full speed…

***

NORTH OF THE VIRGINIA/NORTH CAROLINA BORDER

"I think that's the place," Halle gestured toward a green field bounded on two sides by a variety of buildings. A large rectangle of concrete with three helicopters parked on it—one of them a Blackhawk not too different from their own lay next to one of them.

"I think you're right," Ramnarain looked from the ground to the navigational system. "But I don't see the fueling area..."

"Over there," Halle pointed to a pre-fab building near the parked helicopters. "See the red pump?"

"Put the chopper down as close to that as you can," Ramnarain looked at his watch. "If we do this right, we can be over Washington right in the middle of rush hour..."

"I'll do my best," Halle took a firm grip on the cyclic and began easing off on the collective.

The Blackhawk began to slow...

"This was the hardest part of the simulation," she eased off power. "You have to sort of balance the ship and slowly lower it..."

The ground grew closer.

"Now, if I can just keep things level..." She worked the collective, slowing the ship, dropping it closer to the ground. Closer...

There was a distinct THUD.

"We're down!" Halle turned the motor off. "A little harder than I wanted—but down."

"No problem." Ramnarain unbuckled his seat belt. "Do you see anyone who can refuel us?"

"I don't see anyone at all..." Waterson looked out of the windows on her side of the helicopter. "Shit!"

"What's wrong?"

"That helicopter there," she pointed to the machine closest to the building. "It has FBI markings!"

"No need to panic," Ramnarain put a hand on her shoulder. "I'm sure there are FBI agents all over the country looking for us. Just because one of their helicopters is here…"

"I don't like it." Waterson shook her head. "We should leave now—go somewhere else!"

"We don't have enough gas to get to our target," Halle touched the indicator which showed less than a hundred pounds of fuel. "We'd be lucky to get thirty miles!"

"All right," Ramnarain reached into his bag and pulled out a handgun. "I'll see if there's anyone out there. You look into getting us fuel."

"I'll stay here," Waterson produced a weapon of her own. "If someone does show up to make trouble," she held up her pistol. "I'll puncture the tanks!"

"That'd kill us too," Halle frowned.

"So what?" Waterson's eyes bored into Halle's. "I'm not going to let anyone stop us now!"

She's crazy, Halle thought. They both are! She opened the door on her side of the Blackhawk. They're as obsessed with getting revenge as I am! Jayson's body suddenly appeared in her mind's eye. Am I that crazy?

She wondered as she freed the fuel line and began dragging it toward the helicopter…

***

"They're splitting up," Farrell's voice murmured into Sean's ear. "Looks like one of them is going to stay in the chopper."

"That's Waterson," Sean reported. "She's got a pistol."

"If she punctures the SA canisters while she's on the ground here, it won't reach too many people." The FBI agent-in-charge put in.

"It would, unfortunately," Farrell dead-panned. "Kill all of us."

"Yeah," the FBI man said. "I hadn't thought about that…"

"I could tell!" Farrell shook his head. "Sean, do you or your partner have a shot at Waterson?"

The youngster had joined one of the FBI shooters—an experienced sniper who had positioned them at an angle to the hanger that gave them a clear view of the fuel pump and the chopper that had just landed.

"Maybe." Sean had appropriated a pair of binoculars. Now he had them trained on Ms. Waterson. "As long as she doesn't duck down…"

"We won't give her a chance." Farrell watched as Halle pulled the fuel line to the Blackhawk and began pumping gas. "Agent Gurnie will fire when we take the girl down…"

"You're not going to kill Halle, are you?"

"I don't want to," Farrell sighed. "But I don't really see another way…"

"Okay." Sean turned all his attention to the woman inside the Blackhawk. Ms. Waterson was sitting in the right-hand seat of the passenger compartment, her pistol in her lap, her eyes roving over the helipad area. "I have eyes on Waterson—she has her pistol in her lap—I don't know if it's pointed at the canisters or not…"

At his side, the FBI sniper trained his rifle on the woman in the back of the helicopter.

And flicked his safety off…

***

"Something's wrong!" Ramnarain stopped in his tracks. He'd moved a bit to the right of Halle

204

and was close enough to get a good luck at the FBI helicopter at the edge of the helipad.

A good enough look to see heat rising from its engine compartment.

"Halle!" He turned toward the Blackhawk. "Run for it!"

"FREEZE!" The FBI agent-in-chief yelled the command to the two figures in front of the Blackhawk. "FBI!"

Ramnarain didn't give him a chance to say anything else as he opened fire, his weapon pointing more or less toward the agent-in-chief-- who was forced to take cover.

Inside the chopper, Waterson began firing through the open door, peppering the area around the FBI agents.

"Shit!" Sean heard Farrell curse as the FBI agent in chief came on the line. "Gurnie!" He was a little out of breath. "You are free to engage!

The youngster waited for the M-4 to go off. He was still watching Ms. Waterson who was busily reloading her pistol.

"Gurnie!" The FBI agent-in-chief sounded concerned. "Take the shot!

Sean looked to his right—the FBI sniper was slumped across his rifle, a neat hole in his forehead.

"Gurnie is down," Sean reported, pushing the agent out of the way as he grabbed the man's rifle. "Hit by a stray."

"Roger that." Farrell's voice was calm. "Sean, can you take the shot? I know it's a bit long for a pistol…"

"I have Gurnie's rifle." Sean rested it on a little hummock of grass in front of him. "Acquiring the target now."

Ms. Waterson had reloaded her pistol and was turning toward the back of the helicopter's passenger compartment.

"She's going to release the gas."

"Don't let her do that!"

"I won't." Sean moved the red dot of the rifle's optics until it was aimed right at Ms. Waterson's forehead. She's not a person, he told himself as he took a deep breath. She's nothing but a target. Nothing but cardboard and ink…

He let the breath out slowly… Not a person…

The rifle fired.

CHAPTER TWENTY-EIGHT

They've got us trapped! Ramnarain emptied his pistol into the side of the building the FBI agents had taken refuge behind. *We've got to get out of here!* He slapped a fresh magazine into place.

Halle had already broken into a dead run, sprinting past the FBI position while they were still ducking to avoid Ramnarain's fire. She made it to the gasoline pump, sheltered behind it for an instant, then sprinted for the edge of the hanger.

Farrell rose to one knee and aimed his pistol in her direction—but before he could shoot, Ramnarain emptied his second magazine, bullets spanging off the steel wall of the pre-fabricated building.

Farrell and the FBI team were forced to duck for cover.

Got to get back to the helicopter! Ramnarain put the last magazine into his pistol. *And get away from here!* He made a run for it, trying to keep the FBI chopper between him and the team of agents. He was surprised that he could still breathe normally. *I expected Waterson to release the SA by now!* He looked toward the chopper and saw nothing—no movement, no sign of Waterson...

Maybe she's ducking down to avoid being shot...

A shot panged off the nose of the Blackhawk—missing him by inches. Ramnarain cursed and threw himself through the open door.

"Waterson!" He called out. "Why haven't you..."

His hand touched something wet.

Oh! He chanced a quick look into the passenger area where he saw Ms. Waterson's lifeless body lying across the canisters of SA.

Her head's splattered all over the back window! He searched for the bullet hole, found it in the window opposite the FBI position. There's someone else out there!

He kept down as low as he could and began the process of starting the Blackhawk's engine...

"Stay away!" He yelled out of the window. "If you try to come closer, I'll release the gas!"

The turbines caught as he pulled himself upright and engaged the rotors...

***

Halle darted into the road at the edge of the little airport, than dove into the ditch right alongside it before looking back.

Nobody was following her.

They're all concentrating on the Professor, she realized. I have a chance to get away!

She crawled along the ditch until it ended at another road, than sprinted across that and into a wooded area.

They'll have cops cordoning this whole area off, she told herself. I've got to slip past them. She glanced at the military uniform she was still wearing. To do that, I'm going to have to get rid of these clothes!

She moved through the woods as quietly as she could—and heard multiple gunshots behind her.

The Professor and Ms. Waterson are as good as dead. She told herself. And it's all Sean Piper's fault. Her face went hard. I have to make sure he pays for all of this!

She kept moving through the woods. She was going to get away--she had to get away to get her revenge.

***

Sean saw the rotors on the Blackhawk begin to turn. I can't let him get away with all of that gas! He looked across the field where he knew Farrell and the others were.

None of them were moving.

It's up to me. Sean took a deep breath, checked that his pistol was still in its holster, and cautiously rose to his feet, keeping his head down...

Nobody shot at him.

Ramnarain's busy flying the chopper, he thought. I might be able to make it!

Without another thought, he broke into a run, heading for the helicopter that was slowly lifting from the ground...

***

Crap! Farrell cursed as he saw Sean sprint out of cover. He's going to try to take the damn chopper down by himself! Without a thought, Farrell stood up and began firing at Ramnarain.

"Cover!" He shouted. "Give the kid cover!"

The FBI team responded immediately and bullets began tearing into the front of the slowly lifting Blackhawk.

"He's getting away!" The FBI agent-in-chief stood up and aimed at the belly of the ascending helicopter. "We have to...

Farrell knocked his gun down before he could fire.

"Idiot!" His glare forced the agent to back up a step. "If you had kept your damned mouth shut, we'd have gotten this all done without any trouble. Now..." He gestured to the Blackhawk, now fifty feet up and turning away. "Now we've got to figure a way to bring that down without releasing the gas!"

"The kid got aboard," one of the other agents called out. "I saw him jump into the passenger compartment."

"That's something!" Farrell's eyes continued to flay the hapless FBI agent-in-chief. "Now let's get everyone into our helicopter and chase that thing down!" He motioned toward the FBI chopper. "Now!"

***

Sean managed to get into the passenger section of the Blackhawk just as it was taking off. He rolled right into the mangled body of Ms. Waterson, grimacing as his face smacked into what was left of hers.

Can't let it bother me, he told himself, rubbing blood from his eyes. I've got to get this thing down in one piece! He could see the canisters of gas—two of them under Waterson's sprawling body. Without rupturing any of those!

"Mr. Piper," Ramnarain's voice came from the pilot's seat. "Nice of you to join me!"

"Professor." Sean closed his hand around the butt of his pistol. "Why don't you land this thing before someone gets hurt?"

"You know I can't do that." Ramnarain told him. "I have a debt to pay."

Sean sighed. What do I do now? Do I shoot the Professor and try to land this thing on my own? He had never spent any time on helicopter simulators—he preferred fast movers—fighter jets, space ships—that kind of thing.

"Come on up here in front," Ramnarain patted the seat beside him. "You can keep me company."

Why not? Sean kept his hand on his weapon and climbed into the left-hand seat. I can play for time while I think of something to do...

"That's better." Ramnarain smiled at him. "It's a shame you saw fit to leave us. You'd have been a huge asset."

"An asset you'd have used to kill more people." Sean shook his head. "I saw what happened at Union Station..."

"People are the cheapest commodity on this planet," the older man smiled. "You should know that."

"My father thought..."

"Your father was a foolish man." Ramnarain shook his head. "He thought that he could help those fools in the Middle East even though he knew they've been fighting each other for millennia!" He shook his head. "That's why he's dead. That's why your mother has no income—and why your sister has very little hope of survival."

"You're wrong." Sean looked into the other man's face and caught a glimpse of the insanity there. "He's dead because people like you—intelligent men in positions of authority—believe that human beings aren't important. That they are, as you say, the cheapest commodity on the planet."

"And who's going to punish the people who think like that?" Ramnarain raised an eyebrow. "You?"

"It's not my job to punish them." Sean shrugged. "Just like it's not your job to 'punish' the people of Washington D.C. for what happened to your son."

"You know about that?"

"I know some of it." Sean glanced at the land spread out before him. We're heading north, toward Washington, he realized. If I could get him to move out over the water...

"I know what you're thinking, Mr. Piper." Ramnarain smiled. "And I will not allow this helicopter to get into a position where you can force it down into the water." He tapped his finger on the Cyclic. "One push and we're down in the middle of I-95!" His smile widened. "There are hundreds of little communities on either side of that road—the gas would kill thousands of innocents..."

"I could kill you and take control." Sean told him, tapping his pistol.

"You won't do that, Mr. Piper." Ramnarain smiled. "If that was your plan, you would have shot me already." He looked into Sean's face. "That leads me to conclude that you don't know how to fly a helicopter."

Sean shrugged. "My education has been sadly neglected in that area."

Ramnarain laughed. "It is a shame that I lost you, Mr. Piper. You would have been even more useful that my beautiful Halle." He shook his head. "That idea you had—to marry gaming technology to hacking—that was brilliant!"

"You would've used me for your own ends—just like you used Halle and the others," Sean raised an eyebrow. "And eventually, you would have been forced to kill me as you did poor Mike."

"That was a shame--and a waste." Ramnarain shook his head. "It was completely the fault of that terrible Carole. She wanted money and nothing else really mattered to her. When I didn't give her as much as she expected, she did her best to turn Mike against me."

"So you eliminated him." Sean saw Richmond coming up on his left. Got to make my move soon! "Just like that."

"When it's time to eliminate an adversary…" Ramnarain's left hand suddenly re-appeared—this time with a pistol. "It's best to do it quickly."

CHAPTER TWENTY-NINE

NORTH CAROLINA, 15 MILES FROM VIRGINIA BORDER

Halle had been surprised when the helicopter flew over her. I only got a few pounds of fuel into it—I'm amazed it got off the ground! She watched as the machine headed nearly due north. Maybe the Professor can get more out of it than I could.

Seconds later, a second helicopter went over—following in the wake of the first.

That'll be the FBI, she thought. I wonder if they'll try to shoot it down? She shook her head. That'd be stupid—a lot of people would be killed, but they're government employees so perhaps they wouldn't mind...

She stopped at the edge of a little wooded area. There was a road just ahead—but it was blocked by two County Police cars.

I can't get by them dressed like this; she looked down at her military uniform. And I certainly can't take it off and expect to walk by with no questions asked. She shook her head. No. I have to wait them out. Perhaps they'll leave now that both choppers are gone...

She settled, resting her back against a tree trunk, her eyes on the two cars in the street below...

***

BLACKHAWK HELICOPTER--1000 FEET ABOVE NORTH CAROLINA/VIRGINIA BORDER

Sean had been expecting Ramnarain to make some kind of move—and he was ready. He grabbed the pistol with his right hand and deflected it upward, while, in the same smooth motion, he smashed his elbow into the bridge of the scientist's nose.

Blood spurted as Ramnarain released the pistol and grabbed for his injured nose before slumping in his seat.

The helicopter—uncontrolled—reacted violently, pitching hard left and knocking Sean against the door even as it tossed Ramnarain across the central console and into his lap.

"Sean!" Farrell's voice came through his earbud. "Are you okay? We're just behind you and to your right—what's wrong with your ship?"

The youngster didn't have time to answer—he had other problems. The Blackhawk was bucking and weaving through the sky, the unconscious Ramnarain was stopping him from reaching the controls.

And Washington was not far away.

"Hold one!" Sean took a deep breath and manhandled the limp body of the professor into the rear part of the passenger compartment before switching his own position to the right hand pilot's seat. "I have to ask," he belted himself in. "Do you know how to fly a chopper?"

"Of course," his partner answered. "Why?"

"Because I think I need some help!" Sean swiveled in his chair and smashed the butt of the pistol into Ramnarain's temple, making sure the good Professor would stay down and not bother him.

"How do I get this thing stable?"

"Can you reach the controls?"

"Yeah," Sean stuck the extra pistol into his belt and grabbed for the abandoned controls.

"What seat are you in?"

"Right hand." Sean answered. "Ramnarain's in the back now."

"Okay, take the collective—that's the long bar thing, in your left hand."

"Got it."

"Now take the cyclic—that's the stick in front of you—in your right."

"Okay." As soon as Sean closed his hand around the cyclic, some of the buffeting stopped. "What now?"

"Keep the cyclic nice and steady."

"Trying."

The chopper bucked and tilted hard left, throwing Sean against the straps.

"Sean!"

"Just a minute…" He fought with the cyclic for a long moment and finally got enough of a feel to achieve some semblance of stability.

"There are rudder pedals on the floor in front of you—see if they help."

Sean had used rudder pedals on some of the flight simulators he'd tried in the past so he knew what to do…

"I think I've got it now." Sean said moments later with the chopper flying in a more or less straight line.

"Yeah, I have control," Sean shook his head. "For the moment, at least."

"Good," Farrell kept his voice even. "Now, if you can turn just a little bit to the right…"

Sean nodded and gave the controls all his concentration, turning the cyclic just a hair and using the rudder to shift the helicopter's course…

"Okay, that's good. Now just keep going in as straight a line as you can manage."

"Where am I heading?" Sean asked. He wanted to wipe sweat from his forehead but was afraid he'd lose control of the chopper if he took either hand off the controls.

"The Potomac is only a few miles in that direction. If you can put the chopper down into the water…"

"Put it down!" Sean snorted. "I can barely keep it in the air! How am I going to land it?"

"Who said anything about landing?" Farrell chuckled.

"Oh," Sean gave a quick nod. "I see."

"Nice and level—keep the collective the way it is."

"What happens if I move it?"

"It'll change the pitch of your propellers— which could make you climb or dive, depending on whether you push forward or pull back."

"Swell," Sean wiggled the fingers of his right hand, made sure they weren't gripping the control too tight—he was afraid they'd cramp if he did that for any length of time. "I'll keep that in mind."

"Do that." Farrell paused for a long moment. "You've got about thirty miles to go."

"Roger that," Sean peered through the windshield, searching for the telltale blue of water. "Thirty…"

The helicopter suddenly began to drop earthward, the engine coughing loudly…

CHAPTER THIRTY

15 MILES FROM NORTH CAROLINA/VIRGINIA BORDER

Crap! Halle looked down at the ten foot drop that separated her from the highway. She'd waited until the police cars cordoning off the heliport drove away, then quickly crossed the road and headed east—she knew that eventually she'd cross a main highway where she could get a lift and head for New York.

It's the only way I'm going to be able to get back at Sean, she told herself as she moved through an open field. If I can't find him, I'll go after his mother or his sister...

While waiting for the police to leave, she'd cut the sleeves off her fatigue shirt and removed the various patches and tags. She finished by tying the bottom just under her breasts, making it look like a halter rather than a uniform shirt. More cuts had turned the fatigue pants into rather short shorts.

She was sure nobody would mistake her for a soldier now—not in that outfit.

Now all I have to do, she told herself, is get down there onto the road! She could see traffic and was certain she'd have no trouble getting a lift.

But first I have to get down there. She examined the terrain in both directions. She couldn't see an end to the rise—which left her only one course of action.

I hope no one is watching, she sat at the edge of the drop and put her hands out for support. Because this is not going to be graceful!

She took a deep breath and pushed off, sliding down the near-vertical drop.

The dry red clay crumbled under her heels, slowing her just enough that...

Oof! She hit bottom with enough force to jar her teeth—but not enough to do any other damage...

I seem to be okay, Halle took inventory. She flexed the muscles of her legs. Ankles are okay—knees too. She held her arms up, rotated her shoulders. Nothing broke! She smiled and pushed herself upright. Now all I have to do is find a lift. She brushed red soil from her rear end and headed for the highway, purposely grinding her hips as she went. How hard can that be?

***

BLACKHAWK HELICOPTER--750 FEET OVER SOUTHEASTERN VIRGINIA

"Are you okay, Sean?" Farrell had seen the helicopter dip and wobble before once again settling onto a straight course.

"I think so," the youngster looked around, anxious to find the river. "The engine is missing every now and then."

"Check the fuel."

Sean searched the instrument panel for a long moment before finally identifying the proper gauge. "It reads..." He leaned forward, peering at the unfamiliar instrument. "I think it's telling me that I don't have any fuel at all."

"Okay," Farrell nodded. "We know that Ramnarain was trying to refuel when we caught up with him. I guess he didn't finish." He glanced at the GPS navigator in his own chopper. "We're almost to the river—you'll make it okay." He looked around. "Hold one," he said before tapping the earbud to cut the line. "You!" He pointed at the FBI man in the co-pilot's seat. "Call the Coast Guard and tell them we need a rescue swimmer."

"Sir?"

"That chopper," he nodded toward the front windshield. "Is going to go down. If my partner manages to reach the river, it'll save a lot of lives—and I'd like for one of them to be his."

The FBI man nodded.

"After you reach the Coast Guard, I want you to connect me with Mary Max—you know her callsign?"

"Yes sir." The FBI pilot nodded and began working the controls of the helicopter's radio set.

"Now," Farrell tapped his earbud again, going back on the air. "Still there, Sean?"

"Where else would I be?"

"Okay," Farrell smiled. "We're within ten miles of the river now. You should be able to see it." He looked out his own windscreen. "Right in front of you."

"Not so far," Sean peered out of the windshield. "Nothing out there but a lot of grass and trees."

The engine barked, wheezed—and caught again...

"Engine's getting worse," Sean reported after wrestling the chopper back into level flight. He'd lost another hundred feet of altitude.

"I can tell," Farrell motioned for his own pilot to drop down alongside Sean. "Just keep a gentle hand on those controls. You'll make it."

"I hope you're right," Sean glanced over his shoulder at the three canisters of gas in the rear compartment. "Because if you're not…"

"I'm right, Sean." Farrell kept his eyes on the other helicopter, wondering just how far it could really get.

Then he lied to his partner one more time: "I promise you that I'm right…"

***

15 MILES FROM NORTH CAROLINA/VIRGINIA BORDER

It took less than five minutes for Halle to get a ride—and she immediately realized that it had everything she needed.

Guy's got a laptop; she had seen it sitting on the back seat as she climbed in. A bag of clothes too. She glanced at the middle-aged man as she buckled her seat belt. Maybe he's taking a little vacation?

She wondered.

"So where are you off to, Miss?" The man smiled at her as he flicked his cruise-control on. "I'm going to Philadelphia!"

"I'm heading for New York," she told him. "Meeting some friends there."

"Kind of a long trip to take without any baggage, isn't it?" He raised an eyebrow in her direction. "You sure you're not running away?"

"If I was running away," she turned to look at him. "I'd have baggage, wouldn't I?"

"Maybe so." He nodded. "Anyways, I'll be happy to take you as far as Philadelphia."

Halle pursed her lips, thinking. We'll have to go through Washington if we stay on this road. She glanced at the clock in the car's front panel. If Ramnarain gets through with the gas, that won't be a good thing...

She made a decision.

"Pull over," she nodded toward a rest area just ahead.

"Excuse me?"

Halle produced a knife. "You won't believe this," she grinned. "But I'm trying to save both our lives!"

***

BLACKHAWK HELICOPTER--600 FEET OVER NORTHEASTERN VIRGINIA

Sean finally saw the blue ribbon that he knew was the Potomac River ahead. The engine was really having problems now, backfiring and sputtering as it labored to use every drop of fuel still in its tanks.

It's only a matter of time before it fails altogether, Sean knew. I only hope...

"NO!" A hand clawed at Sean's face. "I won't let you!"

"Professor!" Sean took his hand off the collective and pushed the other man away. "Stop! We'll crash!"

"Good!" Ramnarain rose up between the front seats; his face covered with blood, and made a dive for the controls. He couldn't quite reach them—but his constantly shifting weight was causing the helicopter to bobble up and down.

"Stop moving!" Sean yelled. "It's hard enough…"

"I'll kill you!" Ramnarain suddenly turned on the young man. He threw a week punch at Sean's face—and missed by a foot. "This is all your fault…"

His hand brushed the gun in Sean's belt.

"Don't do it, Professor." Sean grabbed Ramnarain's hand, held it away from the pistol. "I don't want to hurt you…"

"Men like you killed my son!" Ramnarain clawed at Sean's eyes with his free hand. "I will have my revenge!" He grabbed the pistol and yanked it free of the belt…

Sean responded instinctively, pushing the cyclic to the left to bank the helicopter in that direction.

Ramnarain fell backwards and to the side, hitting the door hard.

The helicopter shuddered and the engine coughed before going completely silent for an eternal second…

"I'll kill you!" Ramnarain brought the pistol up toward Sean's face, his thumb searching for the safety…

224

Sean had no choice. He drew his own pistol and put three rounds into the scientist's chest.

Ramnarain recoiled from the impact—and the door, already damaged, suddenly sprang open...

***

"What the hell!" Farrell yelled as he watched Sean's Blackhawk shake and hesitate before banking hard to the left and ejecting a body through a suddenly open door.

"SEAN!"

"I'm okay," the boy's voice came back a long second later. "Ramnarain regained consciousness and tried to shoot me."

"And?"

"I shot him first."

Farrell heard the strain in Sean's voice. "You had to do it. You had no choice..."

"I had no choice with Waterson, either. Or Jayson..."

"Sean, we'll talk about this later. But right now..."

"The engine's really laboring," Sean told him. "I don't believe it's going to run for much longer..."

"The river's only a few hundred yards further. You can start descending."

"How do I do that?"

"Push forward on the Collective—slowly."

Sean did as he was told. "Engine's making more noise."

"That's because you just increased the drag," Farrell told him. "It's okay—see if you can twist the throttle on the end of the collective a bit—feed the engine a little more fuel..."

"Nope," Sean came back. "No change."

"Okay," Farrell looked forward. "The river's right ahead—push the collective down some more—try to keep the chopper as level as you can with the pedals and cyclic..."

Sean did as he said. He saw the river coming up underneath the ship—just as the engine went silent—this time, for good.

God, Sean took a deep breath. It's been ages since I had to swim! He watched the white-flecked water rush at the front of the ship...

Of course, he thought, a wry smile crossing his lips. I might not survive the impact...

An instant later, the Blackhawk hit the Potomac.

The windshield shattered on impact and water poured into the cabin, sweeping up every loose item in the cabin—including Ramnarain's pistol—which flew right into Sean's face.

The youngster had no time to duck and the weapon slammed into his forehead, stunning him for a long moment as the helicopter settled onto its side and began to sink...

"Sean?" Farrell stared at the sinking machine, desperate to find out if there was any movement inside. "SEAN!"

He leaned forward and pushed the door open, searching for some sign of his young partner.

"The Coast Guard?" He asked the man with the radio.

"Ten minutes out."

"Too long." Farrell pulled off his jacket and tossed it on the seat before stepping out of the open door.

CHAPTER THIRTY-ONE

INTERSTATE 95 REST STOP

Halle found a pair of jeans and a t-shirt that could be made to fit her in the driver's bag. She took a moment to boot his laptop, anxious to see what was happening in Washington.

The Professor should have gotten there by now, she told herself, using the driver's cell as a hot-spot for the laptop. One of the News services should be talking about it by now.

There was nothing. Nothing at all.

He failed. She shut the laptop down and tossed it onto the passenger seat. That bastard Piper was able to stop him! Halle took a moment to get her breathing under control. He's got to pay. She started the car, guiding it up the ramp and back out onto the roadway. And I'm the only one left who can make that happen!

Moments later she was on I-95 speeding toward New York City, not giving a single thought to the kindness of the man who had picked her up.

The man whose body would not be found for several hours...

***

BLACKHAWK HELICOPTER--20 FEET UNDER THE POTOMAC RIVER

The water's cold! Sean hated cold water—he'd told his mom and dad that over and over, but they'd always insisted on taking him and his sister to the beach whenever they could—even if it was too early in the season—while the water was icy cold.

Why couldn't we just use the base pool? He'd asked them. The pool is heated so it's nice and warm. He smiled. Nice and comfortable…

Then he remembered the reason they always went to the beach. Dad likes the sounds and smells of the real world—he likes to feel the sun on his shoulders and the sand beneath his feet. Sean's father had smiled as he told his son that.

He had smiled and given Sean a great big hug…

"Sean!" A voice whispered in his ear. "Wake up, Sean."

Dad? He frowned as he realized that he was bent over, looking downward at a floor that was filled with debris of all kinds—even a gun!

This isn't the beach! He realized. Where am I?

He tried to sit up and found that he couldn't. What's on my back? He struggled for a long moment…

"You've got to get yourself free, son. You don't have much time!"

Dad? Sean tried to turn his head. Where are you Dad?

"Come on, boy!" The voice came from somewhere behind him. "I'll help you! On three. One…Two…"

"Three!"

Sean pushed hard—and whatever it was that was pinning him moved. He pushed harder…

And the world snapped back into focus.

Sean looked up at the shattered remains of what had been the Blackhawk's windshield. I'm still inside the helicopter! The seat had me pinned...

A hand touched his shoulder and closed around it while another hand started working on the harness holding him in his seat.

Dad? Sean turned as the buckles holding him in place came free and the hand closed around the front of his shirt and yanked him away from the ruined seat and the wreckage behind it.

He saw Farrell's face—and full recognition of what was happening spread through him as the other man pulled him free of the helicopter.

I'm out of the wreck! He kicked away from the wreckage of the helicopter, fighting the current that was trying to sweep him downstream.

The gas? Sean turned to check on the canisters—but before he could see anything, Farrell grabbed him and began pulling him along.

Toward the light...

Toward the air...

Sean gasped and coughed as the two men broke the surface.

"You okay?" Farrell turned Sean toward him, checking his eyes. "Sean! Are you okay?"

"Ramnarain's gun hit me in the head when I crashed." Sean shook his head. "I guess it knocked me loopy—I had a dream..." He saw the worry in his partner's face. "It's okay," he raised a hand. "I'm wide awake now." He looked around, treading water. "The gas?"

"Below—still in the chopper." Farrell signaled for the FBI men who had landed on shore to toss him a line. He caught it and began to pull the two of them out of the water. "We'll make sure it stays there until we can get a properly equipped crew to salvage it."

"Ramnarain's body?"

"Back there somewhere," Farrell nodded in the direction the chopper had come from. "We'll find it later."

"Did I hurt anyone in the water when I came down?" Sean looked around as they reached the shoreline. Farrell helped him out of the water, dragged him up onto the grass.

"There was nobody out there—and even if there was, your job was to get the chopper—and that gas—into the river." He smiled. "And you did that just fine—as well as anyone could expect you to do."

"Yeah," Sean nodded, face grim. "As well as anyone could expect..."

"Hey," Farrell turned Sean to face him, looked him square in the eye. "You did an incredible job! If Ramnarain had gotten the gas over the city..." He shook his head. "Thousands would have died!"

"And I only had to kill a handful," Sean sighed. "Not many at all."

"Sean..."

"It's okay, Frank." Sean shook the man off and took a deep breath of the air, savoring the feel of it in his sore lungs...

"I'm okay."

He was asleep before the words were out of his mouth.

CHAPTER THIRTY-TWO

WILLIAMSBURG, NEW YORK

This looks like a good spot! Halle parked the stolen car in Brooklyn, not far from the Williamsburg Bridge.

She didn't think it would stay where it was for too long.

Now all I have to do is find a Starbucks.

That didn't take long either, so, a very few minutes later, she was logged onto the internet and hacking her way into a Defense Department site—one she had visited before.

The Professor is dead, she soon learned. So is Ms. Waterson. She searched further. The SA gas is at the bottom of the river with guards mounted on both banks.

She sighed. The HEMO plan was shot to shit—not that it really mattered to her. I didn't care about killing all those people in Washington, she told herself. That was the Professor's hang-up. I just wanted the payment he promised. Enough money for Jayson and me...

Jayson. The thought conjured him up in her mind. Smiling, laughing, touching her...

Bleeding.

Jayson's dead, she reminded herself. And now it's up to me to get even with the bastard that killed him! She turned her full attention back to business. She had the wallet she'd 'liberated' from the kind motorist who had picked her up in Virginia. Now she searched through it, pulling out the credit and debit cards as well as the... She counted. Forty seven dollars in cash.

She logged into the bank that had issued his debit card and typed in the card number.

A password screen popped up.

Okay, she split screens and downloaded a decrypt program from one of the anonymous storage accounts she maintained on the cloud. Let's see just how good his password is!

A moment later, she had her answer.

His birthday? She shook her head. What an ass! She pulled up his account info, determined that he only had a few hundred dollars in his account, and made a note of the password—she'd use it and the card at the first ATM she came upon.

Now for the important part! She searched for information about Sean Piper, digging deep into Defense Department files for basic information, before shifting to New York State files for details.

His mother and sister live way uptown, she found out. Lousy neighborhood. She stared at another bit of information. Sis is going into the hospital soon! She dug further. This might be just the thing! Something akin to a smile crossed her face—a twisted and evil thing that belied her beauty. If I can't get to Sean directly, she nodded slowly. I'll get to him through his family. She logged off the server. After all, he struck at Jayson—who was family to me—it's only fair that I strike him in the same way...

She left the Starbuck's and headed for the elevated train. She had work to do—and only a few days in which to do it.

CHAPTER THIRTY-THREE

Sean woke as sunlight touched his face.

Where am I? He looked around. This isn't that motel they put me in, it's shabbier… He looked up at the overhead tiles and nodded—he'd seen tile like that before.

I'm in some kind of government facility. He decided. But what kind?

"Sean!" The door to Sean's right opened, admitting Frank Farrell. "About time you woke up!"

"What time is it?"

"It's about eight thirty."

"That's not too late…"

"Sean, today's Thursday—you slept around the clock!"

"Oh." Sean pushed himself up, more comfortable when his eyes were level with the other man's.

"It's okay," Farrell waved the time lapse away. "The Doctors tell us that you have a mild concussion—and a pretty nasty collection of bumps and bruises."

"I was in a helicopter crash."

"So you were," Farrell pulled a chair over to the side of the bed. "You should know that we recovered the canisters of SA—they've been returned to the Marine storage depot."

"With someone other than Gunny Crews in charge?"

"That goes without saying." Farrell told him. "We also cleaned out the second bunker—and a

233

third one that we found. It was all prepped and ready for Ramnarain to move again."

"Anything interesting in the computers?"

"Our people are still looking into them." Farrell smiled. "We want you to do the same when you're back on your feet."

"Excuse me?"

"You're one of us now—you have been since that first day in your apartment," the other man smiled. "All this while you've been drawing salary and earning both vacation and retirement credits!"

"So I work for the government, now?"

"I told you that I was recruiting you. You work for me—and Mary Max." Farrell's smile widened. "She's looking forward to seeing you."

"Sure," Sean nodded. "But I'd like to talk to my Mom…"

"I expected that," Farrell handed over a cell phone. "I've arranged for us to see her tomorrow. Mary Max made sure that your Mom and Sister were fully covered by government health insurance. They're going to operate on Kathleen in the morning."

"That soon?"

"Why not?" Farrell shrugged. "By the time Kathleen gets out of the hospital, your Mom will have a nice new apartment for the two of them to live in."

"How…?"

"Mary Max fixed the problem with your Dad's insurance and pension—the fix is retroactive. You mom can afford a proper place now."

"I didn't know killing people was so profitable."

"Only if you kill the right people." Farrell gave him a serious look. "People who are trying to kill innocents…"

Sean sat up straighter, frowning. "Halle!"

"Excuse me?"

"Halle is still on the loose!" He looked at Farrell. "You didn't get her, did you?"

The other man shook his head.

"She's not about to give up just because Ramnarain is dead. She knows she can't reach me, so…"

"You think she'll go after Lisa and Kathleen?"

"Yeah," Sean nodded. "I think she will."

"I have guards posted…"

"She won't go at them that way." Sean shook his head. "She'll use a computer—go through a back door." He threw his legs over the side of the bed. "Get me out of here—I've got to get home right now. Tomorrow might be too late!"

"Yeah," Farrell stood up and headed for the door. "Get your clothes on—I'll arrange your release—and get us transport to New York." He pushed the door open. "If you're right, we don't have a moment to waste!"

***

MORNINGSIDE HEIGHTS—NEW YORK CITY

It didn't take Halle long to get everything she needed to claim her vengeance.

Money was the key—and it didn't take long to get lots of it—with as much more as she needed available as long as she had access to a computer in a city full of ATM's.

With the money in hand, she was able to rent a small apartment near the New York-Presbyterian University Hospital of Columbia and Cornell—the hospital in which Kathleen Piper would have her surgery.

Halle's new place was quite a bit like the one she and Jayson had shared after they'd met and become lovers. That was while both attended Columbia University—not so far away.

And before they met Professor Ramnarain…

No! Halle pushed away the memories. I can't think about that now. She shook her head. I have to have a plan…

She'd first made an attempt to attach herself to the hospital's employment list—she knew that a nurse in a hospital could go anywhere--and a surgical nurse could get involved in all kinds of things…

It was a good plan—but proved impossible-- security was too tight and hospital employment had been frozen. Records of the existing employees had been printed so the guards on duty had full hard copies—complete with photos and fingerprint information—especially the armed guards who guarded the girl's room, the operating theater that was to be used, and the recovery room she'd be taken into afterwards.

Halle didn't think she could get past all of them—and she didn't want to take a chance. There had to be another way.

For a time, she thought about changing the markings on tanks of oxygen and anesthetic so the two would be switched—fatally—in the surgical theater.

That turned out to be unworkable when she found she couldn't get inside.

There was only one thing left.

Halle picked up the phone and dialed a number she had used many times before.

"G?" She asked when it was picked up. "I need a couple of things…"

***

COLUMBIA PRESBYTERIAN UNIVERSITY HOSPITAL
NEW YORK CITY

Again using an FBI helicopter, Sean and Farrell reached the hospital's helipad in less than two hours. They were quickly passed through several layers of security and taken to Kathleen's room.

"Sean!" His mother jumped up when he arrived, rushing to the door to give him a big hug. "We were so worried."

"It's okay, Ma." He smiled. "Mr. Farrell took good care of me."

"I hoped he would," Lisa gave the older man an even bigger hug. "And he arranged all this!"

"That was all Sean's doing," Farrell told her. "He did an incredible job for us—and it was only right for my boss to take care of him." He smiled. "And his family."

"Well, however it happened, I'm just happy that Kathleen is finally getting the attention she needs!" She gave Farrell a big kiss. "I owe you!"

237

"Do you know if this room has Wi-Fi?" Sean asked.

"Why?" Lisa turned toward him. "Are you going to play computer games?"

Sean sat down in the room's lone chair and opened his laptop. "Sort of," he smiled at his Mother. "Frank will explain."

***

A half-mile away, Halle began to make final preparations. The surgery is supposed to start in a half hour—the nurse who schedules the operating theaters will monitor to make sure they're finished on time so they can move forward with the next thing on the schedule. She glanced at the clock on the edge of her desk. She'll update that schedule every ten minutes or so. She tapped a series of commands into her computer. I'll monitor from here and when I'm sure they've taken the girl to the recovery room, I'll move the device into position.

She smiled as updates began to crawl across her screen. It's nice that they're making it so easy for me. Her smile changed, went dark. I'm sure Sean will appreciate the irony when he figures out what happened…

***

"Someone's hit four banks in the last twenty-four hours," Sean reported after a quick sweep. "Not a huge amount of money—but enough…"

"Nobody's reported any thefts," Farrell told him. "I had the FBI check."

"Whoever did this knew just how to hide it from the automatic auditing programs." Sean continued to work the console. "They'll find it when they do a manual audit."

"I'll pass that information to Treasury—they might want to know just how much you know about doing that kind of thing."

"Not as much as Halle," Sean told him. "This is her work."

"How do you know?"

"I saw the programs that Carole and the others used when they hit banks and ATM's." He nodded toward the screen. "None of them were as subtle as this one…"

"I didn't think of Halle as 'subtle'."

"That's because you've never seen her doing what she does best." Sean told him. "Her computer skills are way beyond mine."

"I hope you're wrong," Farrell told him. "Because if that's true, we have no chance to beat her."

They both looked at the empty bed that had held Sean's sister. The sister who was, even know, being operated upon.

"Yeah," Sean turned back to the computer. "I guess I'm just going to have to try harder…"

CHAPTER THIRTY-FOUR

Halle smiled when she noticed someone trying to backtrack her bank 'withdrawals'. This guy isn't bad, she thought. I figured it would take weeks before someone stumbled across my little incursion. She tapped on the edge of her keyboard with a ragged fingernail. I should give him a little gift for being so inquisitive... She considered the various worms and computer viruses she had at her disposal—then glanced at the clock.

No time for any of that now, she realized. The surgery should be almost complete by now. She cleared her screen, forgetting about the unknown who was trying to find her machine. When they take the girl to the recovery room, I'll make my move.

She stood up and walked around the little room, stretching out the fatigue and stress that had crept up on her while she was making her preparations.

Then it will be over. She nodded slowly. Over for Kathleen Piper. Over for her big brother. Her lips compressed into a straight line. Over for me...

***

"Come on, Sean." Farrell put a reassuring hand on his young partner's shoulder. "Your sister is coming out of surgery right now—you've got to be there!"

"Okay," he rubbed at his eyes. "It's just that..."

"What?"

"I almost have a fix on what I'm sure is Halle's computer. I just need a couple of minutes more..."

"Bring the laptop with you—you can sit with Kathleen and your mother in the Recovery room and work from there."

"Yeah!" Sean saved his work, then picked up the computer. "I can do that." He stood up and tucked the machine under his arm. "Is Kathleen okay? How did the surgery go?"

"The Doctor will give us a full briefing in the Recovery room," Farrell told him. "All your mother and I know right now is that everything went well and your sister is doing fine."

"I hope she's okay." Sean followed Farrell out the door. "Mom's been so worried…"

***

She's in Recovery now, Halle smiled as she read the update from the hospital surgical nurse. It's time for me to launch my little surprise. She stood up, leaving her computer logged onto the hospital feed. I'm sure they'll post an update when my package arrives. Halle grinned and opened the window to her apartment, popping the screen free and pulling it inside. That will be my cue to pack up and leave…

The four-rotor drone she was planning to use to deliver her revenge was already assembled and fully charged. She took a moment to attach the C-4 that 'G' had gotten for her, then carefully—very carefully—added a detonator.

All I have to do is run it into the window of the room and… Halle smiled. BOOM! No more little sister!

She picked up the control unit and flipped it on, then activated the drone's engines.

She waited while the miniature rotors spun up to speed...

***

"The Doctor says she'll need one more operation," Lisa told Sean as he entered the Recovery Room. "Just one!"

"That's great Mom!" Sean gave his mother a hug. "Just great!'

"I've been so worried..." She turned to Farrell. "Frank, if it hadn't been for you..."

"Thank Sean," he told her. "He stepped up when we needed him. It was only right that we step up in return."

"You haven't told me much about what happened..."

"It's still classified." Farrell shook his head. "I don't know when that will change."

"It was serious?"

"Very." Farrell nodded. "I can tell you that it if hadn't been for Sean, a lot of people would certainly have died."

"Sean?" Lisa looked at him. "You did all that?"

"Aw, Mom." The young man shook his head, embarrassed. "It wasn't all that big a deal..." He set his laptop on the table and turned it on, then turned back to her. "I did get a chance to visit Dad..."

"You were at Arlington?" Lisa frowned. "How did you end up there?"

Sean glanced at his partner—who gave him a tiny, nearly undetectable shake of the head. "I can't say, Mom—you know how these things go."

"Unfortunately." She stepped to the bedside, gently laid the palm of her hand on her daughter's forehead. "I guess this means you'll be leaving?"

242

"I don't know…" Sean glanced at Farrell again. "It all depends…"

"Sean will be leaving with me," the ex-CIA man said. "But he'll stay in contact—I give you my word on that!"

"How about you, Frank." Lisa looked at him with soft eyes. "Will you stay in contact?"

"Lisa, you know…" He stopped. "What's that noise?"

"I hear it too," Sean stood up. "A loud buzzing…" He crossed the room, opened a set of blinds. "I can't see anything…"

"That's a drone!" Farrell hurried to Sean's side. "Something small with several engines." He leaned down and peered out of the window. "You scan left, I'll scan right…"

"There!" Sean pointed at a dark shape barely visible to the left of the window's centerline. "Is that it?"

"Yup." Farrell frowned. "And it shouldn't be anywhere near the hospital—the FAA passed rules about that."

"It's coming this way." Sean looked at his partner. "You don't suppose…"

"There's something odd attached to the bottom of that thing and I don't want to take any chances!" Farrell turned to Lisa. "Get a nurse in here—move your daughter out of this room!"

"I don't understand…"

"I'll explain later—for now, just do it!" Farrell grabbed the bottom of the window and pulled hard in an attempt to open it. "Thing is painted shut!" He pulled out his pistol. "Sean—get your mother and sister out of here! I'll shoot that thing down before it gets too close…"

"You get them out," he told his partner. "I'm a better shot than you are."

Farrell nodded. "So you are." He stepped back. "Don't hesitate—if it has an explosive payload…"

"I'll hit it as far out as I can." Sean smiled. "I just want to make sure that I don't miss and hit some poor slob two blocks from here by accident."

"You won't," Farrell put a reassuring hand on his shoulder. "I have perfect faith in your abilities."

"Thanks," Sean shook his head. "I wish I had that much confidence."

The drone moved closer, bobbing a little in the updraft from the building.

"Don't wait too long," Farrell turned toward the door where Lisa and a nurse were pushing Kathleen's bed outside. "And for God's sake, don't miss!"

Sean nodded and drew his own pistol. He used the butt to knock out the glass of the bottom window, wincing as the shards dropped into the parking lot below. Hope nobody was down there. He dropped to a knee and rested the front end of the pistol on the window frame. But I can't worry about that now!

The drone was much closer now—less than a hundred yards away.

There is something attached to the bottom of that thing, Sean squinted, trying to make out details. I can't tell what it is…

Fifty yards…

He lined the pistol up, dropped the iron sights into position.

I hope it's not just a camera!

Forty yards...

Sean took a deep breath, released it slowly...

And squeezed the trigger.

**

HALLE'S APARTMENT-MORNINGSIDE HEIGHTS, NY

Halle frowned as the television transmission from her drone disappeared. *I hope I haven't lost control. It would be a shame if...*

A muffled explosion came from outside the apartment—strong enough to rattle the glass in her windows.

Wow! She looked out and saw a cloud of smoke rising from the direction of the hospital. *I think 'G' might have given me a bit too much C-4!*

She headed for her computer, as sirens began to wail in the streets outside. She was anxious to see what sort of information the hospital might be putting out but, when she looked at the screen...

Nothing! She checked her internet connection. *Nothing at all!* She shook her head. *Maybe I disrupted their internet service, I can't think of anything else...*

There was a crash from somewhere behind her and Halle turned to see her front door bounce once as it hit the apartment's cheap carpeting.

Sean Piper stepped inside.

"You!" Halle snarled at him. "How did you find me?"

"Never leave your computer attached to the internet," he smiled and she noticed the cuts on his face. "Not when somebody is looking for you."

"So you found me," she shrugged. "It's too late—I've had my revenge! Your sister…"

"My sister is just fine," he took a long step forward. "We got everyone out of the Recovery Room before your drone got close enough to do any damage." He smiled sardonically. "Especially since I was able to detonate it at a safe distance!"

"Bastard!" Halle grabbed a knife from her desk—a knife very similar to the one Jayson had used—and charged at the young man who had become her nemesis. "I'm going to…"

"You're going to do nothing." Sean held his ground, eyes cold and clear and much harder than they'd ever been before. He waited for Halle to get within arm's length, then pushed the knife aside with his left hand and slammed his open right hand deep into her solar plexus.

Halle fell to her knees, retching and gasping for air.

"I don't usually hit women," Sean told her, closing in. "But for you I'm going to make an exception." He kicked the knife away and took a moment to walk around her struggling form. "Do you know how many people you could have killed with that bomb? Aside from my sister—and my mother…"

Halle glared at him, fighting for air.

"Once upon a time, I thought you were the most beautiful thing I'd ever seen." He shook his head. "But now I know you're nothing but a monster—a heartless creature capable of killing any number of innocent people to get what it wants."

Halle clawed for his leg.

"Get on the floor!" Sean slapped her hand away and put his heel on the back of her neck, forcing her face to the ground. "Stay there!" He turned back to the door. "Frank!"

Farrell stepped in, followed by two New York Police officers. "You didn't kill her?"

"That would bring me down to her level." Sean looked at the woman who was now lying flat on the floor, crying. "Dad would never approve."

"Neither would I," Farrell waved the officers toward the quietly cursing girl on the floor. "I'm glad to see I was right in my assessment of you."

"I'm glad I didn't disappoint."

"Take her downtown," Farrell waved the officers and the now-cuffed Halle toward the door. "I'll be along to collect her in a little while."

He waited until the cops and their prisoner were out of sight, and then turned back to Sean. "Take some time with your mother and sister," he told the young man. "When you're done, give me a call— I'll arrange transport for you."

"Transport?"

"You work for me now." Farrell smiled. "The bigshots above Mary Max signed the final paperwork this morning." He ran a hand down his cheek, frowning at the stubble there. "I'm glad I didn't have to call and tell her I was mistaken about you."

"So I'm in, what, Homeland Security?"

"No," Farrell shook his head. "Officially, you're now in the CIA. Unofficially, you're a member of an elite team tasked with handling cybercrime and criminals that threaten the Homeland." He smiled. "A team that has, at this moment, two members."

"I thought the FBI already had people doing that."

"They do," Farrell shrugged. "They're just not very good at it."

Sean smiled.

"Ramnarain slipped by them without any problem at all—hell, they bankrolled some of his work!" He looked into Sean's eyes. "We can't let that kind of thing happen again."

"So what do we do to stop it?"

"Damned if I know." Farrell smiled. "We're going to have to work all that out as we go along." He turned toward the door. "I'll see you in a week." He looked Sean in the eye. "Bring your laptop" He smiled. "After all; I don't know a thing about computers..."

THE END